Tempus Fugit

Best Wishes

Tempus Fugit

Curt Yengst

MP
Mundania Press

A Mundania Press Production

Mundania Press LLC
6470A Glenway Avenue, #109
Cincinnati, Ohio 45211-5222

To order additional copies of this book, contact:
books@mundania.com
www.mundania.com

Cover Art © 2006 by Trace Edward Zaber
Book Design, Production, and Layout by Daniel J. Reitz, Sr.
Marketing and Promotion by Bob Sanders

Trade Paperback ISBN-10: 1-59426-222-5
Trade PaperbackISBN-13: 978-1-59426-222-7

eBook ISBN-10: 1-59426-223-3
eBook ISBN-13: 978-1-59426-223-4

First Edition • June 2006

Library of Congress Catalog Card Number 2005934680

Production by Mundania Press LLC
Printed in the United States of America

10 9 8 7 6 5 4 3 2 1

Dedication

In loving memory of
Morris Elwood Yengst
1918 – 2004
"Time no longer matters for him now. He lives outside of it."

With special thanks to Dawn, Isabelle, and Miles

"He who gains time gains everything."
—Benjamin Disraeli

Chapter One

Billy Maxwell was furious. He stomped down the stairs of his family's house into the foyer. Had the latch on the screen door been working properly, he likely would have torn it from its hinges as he shoved it open. Instead, it just flopped out of his way. The flimsy door snapped closed behind him as he crossed the front porch and sat with a deliberate thump on the top step.

The house, situated on one of the quiet back roads of the farm town of Cannon Falls, Minnesota, had been in Billy's family for generations. It was a sprawling, two story, farmhouse with a wrap-around porch. Behind it stood an old carriage house that was used as a garage - for more modern carriages. Here and there were vestiges of the property's original use. A rusted plow sat behind the garage, and an old hand operated water pump stood in the middle of the neatly landscaped front yard. It presently served as a centerpiece for a small flowerbed. Much of the original property had been sold to real estate developers decades ago, leaving the house with about an acre of property that bordered a small patch of woods behind it.

The slamming of the screen door aroused the attention of Mrs. Maxwell who stood at the end of the driveway, speaking to a short, dark haired, slender man in a gray business suit. She gave Billy a reprimanding scowl. Shortly, she finished her conversation with the man in the suit, who then climbed into a gray sedan parked at the curb and drove off down the road. She approached Billy.

"Billy, you can slam doors and pout all you like. We've discussed it with everyone involved and it's really what's best for Uncle Will."

"Yeah, whatever," Billy retorted, shifting his eyes. "I can't believe you're doing this."

This was the family's decision to send Uncle Will to the county hospital for "tests." He had always been eccentric to a certain extent; but in recent years, he seemed to make less and less sense to most of the family. On a number of occasions, he would disappear into his basement workshop for hours and emerge wearing different clothing, and even uniforms of various kinds. On other occasions, he would enter the workshop only to be seen moments later in the yard, acting suspiciously.

Sometimes he would appear outside in the coldest weather without a coat. He had even been observed, more than a few times, walking along the road, miles from home, having told no one where he was. Once or twice, the police had gotten involved. Through it all, Uncle Will remained uncharacteristically tight-lipped about his activities.

The last straw came when Billy's parents decided to sell the house and its remaining property and move closer to the Minneapolis area. Uncle Will became quite irate and threatened to do whatever it took to prevent the sale of the house. When pressed on the issue, he consistently refused to give any valid reasons. He simply said he needed more time; but for what he wouldn't say. At present, he was refusing to leave the house, even briefly, for any reason. His sister and the others feared that he was slipping, perhaps experiencing a mental breakdown at the possibility of leaving the only home he'd ever had, or some other mental illness. It was unclear to most people whether he lived with his sister's family or his sister's family lived with him. The family resorted to professional intervention. They finally convinced him to admit himself to the hospital for tests.

"Billy," his mother said, "we've been over it a thousand times. Do you think it's easy watching my own brother slowly lose touch with reality? He talks about people nobody knows and places he could not possibly have been, and..."

"So what, Mom!" Billy interrupted. "It's not like he's dangerous or anything like that. Maybe he's just getting forgetful in his old age."

"Billy, he's only a few years older than I am. Besides, you're making it sound like we're dragging him away in a straight jacket. It's just for some tests. He'll be back in a few days. I only care about his well being. We all do."

"Oh yeah?" Billy rose to his feet. "I think this whole family has lost touch with reality!"

With that he stormed down the steps, across the yard, and finally along the road.

"Billy, you get back here right now!" His mother's order went unanswered.

With that, Mr. Maxwell appeared at the front door. Steve Maxwell was a tall, thin, plain looking man in his early fifties. He was a cabinetmaker by trade. He absent-mindedly picked at a tiny splinter in the palm of his right hand. While his expression appeared passive, almost sleepy, his eyes hinted at slight annoyance. Steve was the kind of person with a very long fuse.

"Carolyn, don't say I didn't tell you. He wasn't going to jump for joy over this."

"What am I supposed to do, Steve?"

Carolyn Maxwell leaned her petite frame against the doorpost. Steve nudged the screen door open and placed his hand on her shoulder, brushing aside her dark brown hair.

"Just let him walk it off. Once he comes back, I'll talk to him. He's going to take it hard for a while. As close as he is to Will, it's not surprising."

Indeed, from the time he was a baby, Billy had always been close to his uncle; he was named after him. Uncle Will lived in part of the downstairs portion of the house. He also used a large part of the basement as a sort of workshop. The family never entered his workshop unless admitted by him, which was a very rare occasion. There he tinkered with innumerable gadgets, which littered the entire room. He spent nearly all his time there, which often intrigued the family; since, although he always had plenty of money, he appeared to have no visible source of income. When asked, he would simply claim to be a dealer of antiques. Some of his wares were even displayed throughout the rest of the house. But, most of his collection consisted of what Carolyn referred to as "all that junk."

He would often entertain his favorite nephew with stories of how he came into possession of such treasures, how he traveled to some far-flung locale or another. Carolyn was always quick to pull Billy aside and tell him that they were probably fakes, purchased through a mail order catalog, or even fabricated by Uncle Will himself.

Billy was not unlike the average fifteen-year-old. He participated in sports and music, thought about cars, and of course, girls. He wore his dark brown hair longer and his clothes sloppier than his parents preferred. But, at the same time, he got good grades, helped around the house, and was active in his church's youth group. He also respected his elders, usually, especially his Uncle Will. It was going to be tough getting used to him not being around. As he approached the street corner a half a mile from his house, he heard a voice to his left, calling his name. He turned to see his best friend Nik, riding his mountain bike. Nikolai Brenitski was the son of Russian immigrants who had come to America following the break-up of the Soviet Union and the hard financial times that followed. Although Nik's English was excellent, he spoke with a noticeable accent. The two had met years ago at youth group.

"Hey, Billy, what's wrong? You look like somebody died!"

"It's my Uncle Will."

"Your Uncle Will died?"

"No, No! He's fine. It's just that my parents are trying to have him committed."

"I'm not sure I understand," Nik raised an eyebrow. "Committed to what?"

"A mental hospital," Billy explained. "They want to put him in a mental hospital. They say he's become irrational and delusional and stuff like that."

Nik's expression turned grave.

"Is he really, how do you say, losing his marble?"

"Marbles. He probably lost them years ago. But who cares?! So he tells a few far out stories once in a while and gets dates mixed up. That's no reason to put him away." Billy tried to change the subject, "Where were you headed anyway?"

"I was going to your house," Nik said as he dismounted his bike.

"Good. I sort of shot my mouth off before I left there. My parents will probably be less likely to yell at me about it if you're around."

The two walked back toward Billy's house. When they arrived, they saw Steve sitting on the front porch in a lawn chair holding a coffee mug. He smiled knowingly at Billy, who hung his head and looked away.

"Billy," his father called, "come here for a second, please. I need to tell you something."

"Here it comes," Billy muttered to Nik. "Wait for me back by the garage, okay?"

"Good luck," Nike replied jokingly.

Billy ascended the front steps and stood, leaning against the post.

"Look Billy," his father began coolly, "I don't appreciate the way you stormed out of here before, but that's not what I want to talk to you about. It's your Uncle Will..."

"I thought Mom said it was all settled," Billy interrupted.

"Please let me finish," Steve said, raising his hand. "Your mother and I talked about this while you were gone. You seem concerned that Uncle Will's affairs will somehow be mishandled, like we're going to pack him off to a nursing home or something like that."

"'Funny farm' is more like it."

"Well, we assure you that's not going to happen. Now, I have an idea I want to run past you. We'll have to discuss it with Uncle Will as a family, but I think he'll go along."

"Okay." Billy's mood began to lighten. He could usually tell when his father was about to make his day. "What's the plan?"

"We're going to put you in charge of Uncle Will's part of the house while he's in the hospital. Anyone who wants access to that part of the house has to go through you. What do you say?"

Billy thought about it for a moment. It wasn't entirely what he wanted. He really wanted Uncle Will to stay home and not have to deal with this, but this was certainly the lesser of two evils.

"All right," Billy nodded, "we'll see what Uncle Will says."

"Good enough."

Billy strode down the front steps and around to the garage where Nik was waiting. Nik looked up expectantly.

"How did it go?"

"Pretty good," Billy replied. "Let's go down to the school to shoot some hoops and I'll tell you all about it."

Billy took a basketball from the shelf just inside the garage door, and the pair headed down the driveway to the road.

Chapter Two

After a dinner of fried chicken, mashed potatoes, and corn on the cob, Carolyn Maxwell cleared the table with the help of Lydia, Billy's thirteen-year-old sister. She was basically a slightly smaller version of her mother in appearance, but with a much more playful, inquisitive demeanor. Steve was in the living room, relaxing in his large, brown recliner, as was his custom after dinner. Billy sat on the end of the sofa, which stood opposite Steve's chair.

Carolyn and Lydia came in from the kitchen. Carolyn sat in a small side chair in the corner of the room. Lydia sat on the floor in front of Steve's chair and leaned against his knee.

"Lydia, you have homework to do, don't you?" her father asked.

"Did it already," she said with an expectant smile.

"Then find something else to do," Carolyn ordered. "This doesn't involve you."

"Mom," Lydia whined, "I never get to do anything! Billy's always put in charge of things."

"Lydia, don't argue with your mother," Steve interrupted. "We've already discussed it."

"Don't worry, Lydia," Billy muttered. "When Mom loses her marbles, you can be in charge!" His eyes darted around the room in a desperate attempt to avoid eye contact with either of his parents.

"All right," Steve decided to nip the upcoming argument in the bud. "Billy, are you OK with what we discussed before?"

As Billy nodded, the creaking of the basement stairs announced the appearance of Uncle Will.

Uncle Will, or William Sheppard, as he was known outside the family, was a stocky man in his early fifties. He had dark, receding hair and a goatee, which had traces of gray in it. Much of the time he wore a brown cardigan sweater. He also wore a pair of thin wire-framed eyeglasses that constantly slid down his nose. A pair of worn-out, canvas sneakers peeked out from under his baggy trousers. He pursed his lips and scanned the room, looking as though he had walked into something that was none of his business.

"Are you going to give Billy the key?" Carolyn asked.

Uncle Will scratched his beard and eyed Billy pensively for a moment.

"How old are you now, boy?"

"Fifteen."

"Hmm, fifteen. I guess you're old enough to handle it," Uncle Will said, reaching into his pocket. He almost imperceptibly raised an eyebrow, as if something had just occurred to him. He withdrew an empty hand from his pocket.

"Come with me downstairs, Billy."

Billy rose from the sofa and followed Uncle Will down the hallway. Lydia jumped to her feet to follow as well, and this stopped Uncle Will dead in his tracks.

"Just Billy," he admonished, much to Lydia's disappointment. Her parents echoed his sentiments, much to her extreme disappointment.

"You worry too much, boy," he told Billy as they descended the stairs. His tone was gruff, but jolly. "This is just temporary. Once your mother figures out what a waste of everybody's time this is, things will be back to normal."

"I just don't understand why you're going along with it," Billy replied.

"Well, let's just say I'm humoring her. Besides, it'll be fun playing head games with those idiots," Uncle Will said with an obvious hint of disdain.

"They'd have to get up pretty early in the morning to get one over on you, huh?" Billy chimed.

"They'd have to stay up all night!" Uncle Will retorted.

Once Billy and his uncle reached the basement, they approached the heavy, wooden door to the workshop. Uncle Will turned back to make sure they were not followed. Once he was certain, he took a key from his pocket and unlocked the door. Billy's eyes widened as the door swung open and Uncle Will ushered him into this sort of inner sanctum. The room was larger than Billy had remembered. It had been years since he'd been in there. The room was a jungle of boxes and crates of all sizes. Tools were hanging on a large pegboard at one end, but still more tools were scattered throughout the room. Other objects hung on the walls and littered the table and workbench. Everything had a thin sheen of dust on it. The opening of the door had raised a cloud in the middle of the room, and the particles swirled in a beam of sunlight coming in from the window as the sun set behind the house.

As Billy's eyes scanned the workshop, various objects caught his attention. One item was a large white ring hanging on the wall, on which were printed the words "RMS Titanic." In one corner sat a trunk with its lid open. Inside were some pieces of shiny, twisted metal. A small paper tag hung from the handle of the trunk. On the tag was written "Roswell, N.M. 1947." As Uncle Will carefully closed the door behind them, Billy noticed a photograph hanging on the back of the door. It was of a tall man with short, dark hair and a thin mustache, standing next to an airplane. Across one corner of the picture, a quick hand had written:

Thanks for all your help, William.
Best of luck to you.
Howard Hughes.

"Come here, boy. Sit down," Uncle Will beckoned, placing a small stool in front of Billy. He then began to look for something for himself to sit on. Spotting a milk crate full of old tools, he upended it, spilling the tools on the floor with a great crash. He giggled at the noise. He would have taken a chair. There were four of them around a small table, but they were all holding boxes of junk.

"What's with the sneaking around before, making sure we weren't followed?" Billy asked.

"Got something for you."

Uncle Will sat on the crate, directly across from Billy. He reached into the pocket of his worn out sweater and pulled out a large gold pocket watch with a short fob chain. It glistened in the orange glow of the setting sun. The watch had a hunting case, the kind with a flip-open cover, but it was larger than most watches. He handed it to Billy, whose eyes shone with amazement. Billy examined the watch. It felt heavy in his hands. It was ornately engraved; but the most interesting feature of the case was what was engraved on the cover. It was a picture of a banner bearing the words "*Tempus Fugit.*" He pressed on the stem to flip open the cover. The face of the watch had a white enamel surface with large Roman numerals. There was a moondial just below the twelve, and a small oval window just to the left of the three, showing the date, month, and year.

What Billy saw on the inside of the cover intrigued him the most. It was completely covered with a red, ruby-like, flat crystal that twinkled in the light. It seemed to have a depth to it beyond what the watch cover would allow. Inlaid in the center of this small sea of red was what appeared to be a small diamond. The light that reflected from objects in the room seemed to dance inside this gem and dissipate into the red crystal. Billy found it hard to take his eyes off it. He gave the stem a turn and the watch began to tick hypnotically.

"Here, let me show you something," Uncle Will said.

He walked toward the window, and Billy followed, looking over his shoulder. Uncle Will pulled the stem of the watch and began to change the date. He pointed the inside cover of the watch toward the beam of sunlight coming through the window. The sunlight began to shimmer and sparkle in the crystal surface, and soon it was reflecting a spectrum of colors into the room and against the wall. Billy blinked in amazement. He could feel the hairs on the back of his neck standing up, and his ears began to ring ever so slightly. What happened next shocked him. The rays of light emanating from the watch cover began to form a circle several feet in diameter in the space just before the window. The circle of light swirled and pulsated in flashes of color. Suddenly, it occurred to Billy that the ringing he heard was not in his ears. He glanced at Uncle Will, who was laughing with delight. He looked back toward the circle to find that it was beginning to collapse, until what remained was a large black hole suspended in space between them and the window. Billy was aghast. His heart was pounding. He looked back at Uncle Will, who snapped the cover of the watch shut and put the watch back in his pocket, grinning mischievously all the while.

"Come on, boy!" he half shouted, grabbing Billy by the arm and walking toward the hole.

"What the heck is that thing?!" Billy gasped, resisting fiercely.

"Not to worry. This won't hurt a bit."

The pair continued to move toward the hole. Billy looked apprehensively at the edges, wondering what unseen force held them in place. As he met with the black void, he blinked instinctively.

When he opened his eyes, he saw the window through which the sun shone. He noticed that there was less dust in the air. He turned around to find the room much cleaner than it was a moment before. Also, many of the things in the room were gone. Uncle Will walked to the door and put his ear to it. He then opened it slowly and waved to Billy to follow him, placing a finger to his lips. They slid across the basement, which also looked very different, to the stairs. Upon reaching the top of the stairs, Uncle Will carefully opened the door barely an inch and peered through it. He then invited Billy to look as well.

What Billy saw froze him with horror. He opened his mouth, but no sound came. Down the hallway from the basement door, he saw his mother in the living room. At least he knew it was his mother, because he knew what she looked like years ago. She looked much younger, with a hairstyle she hadn't worn for quite some time. She was dusting furniture they had gotten rid of years before. What horrified him even more was what he saw next. At his mother's feet was a pre-school aged Lydia. Lydia was supposed to be thirteen years old! Billy withdrew from the doorway, turning paler by the moment. Uncle Will grabbed his arm to steady him and helped him back down the stairs and into the workshop.

"Wh...What's going on, Uncle Will?! What did you do to them?!" Billy finally managed to sputter between gasps of breath.

"I didn't do anything to them," Uncle Will replied. "They're fine."

Billy glared at him in shock.

"You are crazy!" he squealed.

"Billy, I'm surprised. I thought you had more respect for your uncle than that."

"Well, what's going on then?"

Uncle Will took the watch from his pocket again and began to explain.

"It's time travel, Billy. The watch makes it happen." He held the watch open in front of Billy. "You set it for which year you want to go."

"This can't be happening," Billy sputtered. "It's just..."

"Crazy?"

Billy stood gaping, as Uncle Will continued to explain.

"It's limited to only about two hundred fifty years."

"Where did you get that thing?!" Billy was starting to calm down.

"I came across it years ago, through an old friend, you might say," Uncle Will explained. "You see, I haven't done as much traveling as most people think. At least not in the usual sense."

"So all this stuff..." Billy gestured toward the empty room. He suddenly remembered that most of Uncle Will's junk was gone. Uncle Will could see he was becoming disoriented.

"Here, boy. Let's get back to where we belong," he said, holding the open watch in the sunlight. "Or should I say 'when?'"

Presently, they were back in the workshop as they had left it moments before, littered with junk, tools, and dust. Billy was still quite shaken.

"Okay, Uncle Will, what's the catch?"

"The catch is that this is our secret. You are not to tell anyone. You got it?"

"Oh, absolutely! They can tear my fingernails off. I won't tell," Billy asserted. "Besides, who would believe it?"

"My feelings exactly."

Uncle Will tossed the watch toward Billy, who caught it clumsily.

"Keep it, boy," he said, "I've had enough fun with it."

Billy looked at his uncle with astonishment, then looked at the watch, then back at his uncle.

"I...I..."

"Relax, Billy," Uncle Will reassured, "I think you're level-headed and mature enough to handle it, or I wouldn't have agreed to...oh, that reminds me." He reached into his pocket and took out the key to the workshop, handing it to Billy.

"Thanks, Uncle Will," Billy said, clipping the key to the other end of the watch's chain.

"Thank *you*, Billy," his uncle replied, turning to leave the workshop. "Remember, time flies!"

Chapter Three

The days that followed were most nerve wracking for Billy. He knew he had to keep quiet about the watch, but he was practically bursting at the seams to tell someone. A few times, he had considered using it, getting as far as staring at that large black hole, only to lose his nerve at the last moment. He wondered why Uncle Will had even given him the watch in the first place. Nik had noticed the change in Billy's demeanor; and, that Saturday, while the two sat on Billy's front porch, Nik decided to bring up the matter.

"Billy," he asked, "is something bothering you? You just have not been yourself lately."

Billy scratched in the dirt with a stick, briefly considering the course he was about to take.

"Nik, what I have to say is something I'm not supposed to say."

"I am not sure I understand."

"I've been sworn to secrecy."

"I see."

"But," Billy stood up, "if I don't tell someone, I'm going to go nuts. So, I might as well tell you."

With that, Billy entered the house, beckoning for Nik to follow. The two walked quietly down the stairs to the basement. Billy reached into his pocket and took out the watch. When they had reached the door to Uncle Will's workshop, he took hold of the key at the end of the chain, unlocked the door and the pair entered the workshop. Nik had much the same reaction to the surroundings as Billy had. After letting his eyes scan the room, Nik finally looked at Billy, who stood cradling the watch in his hand.

"Where did you get the watch?" Nik asked.

"That's the secret," Billy began. "It's a gift from my uncle."

"Okay." Nik replied, with a look on his face that said, "So what?"

"You're never going to believe this," Billy paused, clutching the watch tightly. "What would you say if I were to tell you that this watch does more than just tell time?"

"Get to the point, Billy," Nik said impatiently.

Billy paused one last time, as if trying to find one last alternative.

He really couldn't find one. Nik was the closest friend Billy had. He could also be trusted. Billy certainly could not tell his parents; they would certainly relieve him of such a prize. He also could not trust Lydia to keep quiet about it. There were only two people in the world Billy knew he could trust with such a thing. One of them was presently in the hospital, and the other stood before him.

"Nik, you have got to promise me you won't tell anyone about this."

"Billy, you have my word. Now what is this horrible secret?"

"I'm serious, Nik."

"Sorry, Billy," Nik smiled. "Seriously, you can tell me. I won't say a thing to anyone."

"The watch," Billy began cautiously, "can let you travel through time."

Nik's expression did not change. He just looked at Billy as if expecting him to explain further what he was talking about.

"This is the big, deep, dark secret?"

Billy let out a heavy sigh of exasperation.

"I knew you wouldn't buy it!"

"Well, Billy, what did you expect? That is the most ridiculous thing I have ever heard."

"OK, fine," Billy retorted, "I'll prove it to you."

Billy walked out of the workshop, again beckoning Nik to follow. They went up the stairs and out the back door. When they had reached the back of the garage, Billy looked around carefully to ensure they were not observed. He took the watch from his pocket, flipped it open, and aimed it at the sun. Nik looked on in amazement, especially at the jeweled underside of the lid, which now splashed light and color onto the drab, wooden siding on the back wall of the garage. His amazement turned to terror as the dark hole appeared.

"I've always wanted to see what my grandpa was like as a kid," Billy said, "to see if all the things Uncle Will told me were true."

Nik stood motionless, his mouth hanging wide open. Billy grabbed him by the arm.

"Let's go!"

"Wh...Where?!"

"Not where, when. 1957 to be exact."

Nik and Billy disappeared into the hole.

When they emerged on the other side, they were standing near a huge oak tree that stood at the opposite edge of the back yard, far from the garage. The garage had a fresh new coat of paint. The house looked much the same. As Billy peered around the corner, he saw, sitting in the driveway, a shiny, new, cream-colored 1957 Ford Thunderbird, the exact one he had seen pictures of in the family photo album. Billy turned around and motioned to an extremely startled Nik to proceed to the far end of the garage to a footpath that led into a small patch of trees. Once there, Billy crouched on the ground at the base of a large tree.

"There, we made it." He whispered. "Now, if we follow this path through the woods, we should come out at the back of the old school yard. That's where my uncle used to play—I think."

Nik paced nervously, muttering in his native Russian.

"Nik, relax," Billy assured. "We can go back as easily as we got here."

"Where is here?!" Nik spat, his eyes wide with terror.

"My yard, but fifty years ago," Billy explained. "I told you it worked!"

Billy rose up and began to walk toward the clearing at the far end of the woods. Nik collected himself somewhat and followed. As they entered the clearing at the back of the schoolyard, they could see a group of children playing in a sandbox near some swings and a sliding board. They continued to walk toward the school building. As they drew closer, they noticed two adults sitting on a park bench, feeding a small flock of pigeons with breadcrumbs. In the street, they noticed a few cars parked at the curb, their heavy steel bodies and abundance of chrome revealing the time period. One of the cars had the characteristic markings of a police car. The officer sat at the wheel, eating a sandwich.

Billy and Nik finally reached the playground and stood to survey the area. What immediately caught their attention was the fact that everyone, including the children, was staring at them. After a moment, one of the adults, a woman, stood up and walked over to the police car. Billy paid close attention to this woman as she mumbled to the policeman that she didn't like the looks of those two strange young men, and how she was sure they weren't from around here anyway. With that, Billy looked at Nik, and for the first time, realized that they were the only males in sight with long hair.

"Uh, oh," he muttered, as he saw the cop getting out of his car, eyeing them cautiously.

"Let's get out of here," Nik pleaded. The words had scarcely left his lips, when the two boys turned and sprinted back toward the woods.

"Hey you two! Get back here!" the cop shouted as he gave chase.

The boys crashed through the underbrush. Billy tried furiously to get the watch out of his pocket. In no time, they were back in Billy's yard, or what would someday become Billy's yard. Billy fumbled with the stem of the watch, setting it for the date they left. Nik goaded him to hurry. The pounding footsteps of the policeman were getting closer. Billy placed the cover in line with the sun; and after what felt like an eternity, the hole appeared, and the two disappeared, leaving the befuddled policeman wandering fruitlessly in the woods.

Chapter Four

The next day was Sunday; and as was their custom, the Maxwells were in church. Billy sat with Nik and a small group of other boys in a pew toward the back. His parents sat in front of them, along with Lydia. As the pastor announced the next hymn, the congregation stood to sing. Billy and Nik rolled their eyes in boredom. Nik began to mimic one of the deacons, who was known for his dour expression, much to Billy's amusement. Billy's eyes scanned the congregation. He found another individual holding a hymnal high in front of his face, singing loudly off key. Billy started to do likewise, which caused Nik to nearly double over, trying to suppress his laughter. The entertainment came to an abrupt end when Billy's father turned around and thumped Billy on the shoulder, sternly glaring at him. His mother gave him an equally angry look. Lydia just smirked with much satisfaction.

After the hymn, everyone was seated. Billy reached into his jacket pocket and removed a scrap of paper. He nudged Nik with his elbow and motioned as if to write. Nik unzipped the leather case in which he carried his Bible and took out a ballpoint pen, handing it to Billy. Billy scribbled on the paper and passed it to Nik:

"I'll probably get chewed out for that one."

Nik wrote back:

"Stop making me laugh or you'll get me in trouble! I don't know how I'm going to stay awake through the sermon. I didn't sleep a wink last night."

"Why not?"

"You tell me! It's not every day a person travels back in time and almost gets arrested!"

"I've got to talk to my uncle about this. We're supposed to go visit him after church."

And so they continued to pass notes until the sermon was over. Everyone rose to leave.

"Billy, I don't want to see that kind of behavior again," his mother scolded, waving an index finger in his face. "You should know better!"

Billy was trying hard not to laugh, and doing a poor job of it. His father stepped in as they made their way out the door and toward the car.

"Billy, you're not going to think it's a bit funny when you spend the rest of the week in your room."

"But Dad..."

"But nothing! You're fifteen years old. Start acting like it."

The Maxwells piled into the car, Billy waved good-bye to Nik, and the family headed for the county hospital.

The hospital was located a few miles from the center of town on several acres of neatly landscaped land, with several patches of trees separated by wide expanses of grass and flowers. The hospital itself was a newer brick building with narrow windows and heavy stone pillars framing the entrance. It looked more like an office building located in the middle of a park than a mental hospital. The Maxwells met Uncle Will in the large main foyer of the building. He was sitting in an armchair, accompanied by an attendant. After about an hour of conversation that consisted mostly of small talk, Uncle Will stood.

"Well now, if you will all excuse us, I'd like to speak to Billy for a few minutes."

Billy's parents looked at Uncle Will inquisitively, then at each other. Finally, they decided to go down to the hospital cafeteria for some lunch, with Lydia in tow. Billy and his uncle walked through a side exit to a footpath on the grounds.

"So tell me, Billy," Uncle Will began, "have you had a chance to use the watch?"

"That's what I want to tell you about," Billy explained. "Nik and I went back to..."

"NIK and you?!" Uncle Will half shouted with a sarcastic grin, "I knew it."

Billy panicked. The last thing he wanted to do was upset his uncle.

"I'm sorry, Uncle Will. I just couldn't help it. It was driving me..."

"Nuts?"

Billy continued to fidget and shift his eyes in guilt.

"I only told Nik. He's the only one I'd trust."

"Well," Uncle Will responded, "I should have expected as much. An old friend of mine once said that three men can keep a secret if two of them are dead." He placed a reassuring hand on Billy's shoulder. "If you trust him, then I guess I can too."

The two continued down the path. Coming to a park bench, they sat down.

"You started to tell me about your 'trip,'" Uncle Will said.

"Oh, right," Billy started. "We went back to 1957; but some weird things happened. First, everyone looked at us like...like..."

"Like you weren't from around there."

"Right. But we figured that out. We just didn't look like your typical 1950's teenager. But that's not the strangest thing. When we left, we were behind the garage. When we got to 1957, we were on the other side of the yard."

"Ah yes," Uncle Will remarked, "that's something I forgot to mention - orbital displacement."

"Orbital displacement?"

"Yes. It's hard to explain without a long, drawn out physics lesson. You see, the earth's rotation slows down by very, very minuscule amounts over very long periods of time. The earth also wobbles a little on its axis. When you go back in time, you may not necessarily end up in the exact same spot. Just the fact that the earth rotates is enough to make it happen. For example, the spot where we're standing right now was actually somewhere else in space ten years ago, and somewhere else still twenty years ago."

"I think I get it," Billy nodded.

"Bear in mind," Uncle Will continued, "the time you travel to will always affect where you end up."

At that moment, a pair of attendants approached followed by a tall, middle-aged man in a brown tweed jacket. He was completely bald and wore a short goatee. His eyes were a piercing shade of pale blue. Billy barely noticed a look of dread that flashed across Uncle Will's face for an instant. The bald man spoke.

"Mr. Sheppard, we were told we might find you here. I'll be taking charge of your case. I am Dr. Janus."

"Yes I know," Uncle Will muttered through a stiff expression. "We've met before."

"Have we?" Dr. Janus asked, with a hint of sarcasm. "I don't think so. Well, I was told to expect this. I'll have to ask you to come with us. Your guest will be escorted out"

With that, one attendant stood over Billy and motioned for him to follow. The other grasped Uncle Will's arm and lifted him to a standing position. It seemed to Billy that the attendant was using more force than was necessary. As the attendant and the doctor led Uncle Will away, he turned to look back at Billy.

"Don't forget your Bible lesson, Billy. Ephesians 5:16."

Billy looked at his uncle with a pained expression, having no idea what he was talking about. The old man responded with a wink.

"Ephesians 5:16."

Chapter Five

Billy and Nik sat in the workshop, staring into space. Billy had just finished relating to Nik all of what had happened at the hospital.

"My uncle's in trouble. I knew that doctor didn't look right."

"This is very bad," Nik's Russian accent became thicker, which happened when he was concerned or nervous. "Do you really suppose he is in danger?"

"What else am I supposed to think?" Billy responded. "That Dr. Janus gave me the creeps the minute I saw him. There was just something about him. Something..."

"Evil?" Nik asked, trying to finish Billy's thought.

Billy nodded emphatically.

"I wonder what he meant by the scripture reference," Nik said, "Ephesians 5:16."

"I don't know," Billy answered, "but it should be pretty easy to find out."

With that, he went to the bookcase at the far end of the workshop and found a large, well-worn, leather Bible. He opened it to Ephesians 5:16 and read aloud:

"Redeeming the time for the days are evil."

Billy looked at Nik, who looked back at him, wondering what to make of it. Billy reread the passage. Something unusual caught his eye; not the words themselves, but what was on the page with them. Certain letters were underlined in ink:

"Redeeming the time for the days are evil."

Billy leafed through the Bible to see if any other passages were marked like this; but he found none.

"Maybe it is some kind of coded message," Nik proposed.

Billy rolled his eyes. "Nik, this is serious. We're not talking about spies and cloak-and-dagger type stuff here. It's just my uncle."

"Fine, fine," Nik retorted. "What do I know?"

"I guess it's possible," Billy shrugged. He brought the Bible to the table, collecting a sheet of paper and a pencil from the workbench.

They decided to start with what seemed obvious enough, writing down only the letters that were underlined.

"R E M T H E M F O R D S A E V"

"Now," Billy said, "I guess we have to unscramble them into some kind of secret message."

The pair worked for a short while, scribbling the letters in different order again and again, using up several more sheets of paper, until they came up with what seemed to make only a bit of sense.

"S A V E M E F R O M T H E D R"

After looking intently at it for a moment, Billy's eyes widened as the sentence suddenly made sense. He read it aloud: "Save me from the doctor."

The two boys stood with gaping mouths over the sheet of paper. After a long silence, Nik spoke.

"He is in danger."

"He's got to be," Billy replied, "I don't know how he got this message to me, but I've got to do something."

"But what?"

"That's just it. I don't know."

The two lapsed back into silence as they tried to think of a solution. Again, Nik broke the silence.

"Is there some way to use the watch to help him?"

This got Billy's mind caught up in a whirlwind of possibilities.

"That's it!" he half shouted. "We could go back to just before he went to the hospital, and then we can sneak him into the basement."

"Billy," Nik replied with hint of doubt, "I don't think that will work."

"Why not?"

"First, if we go back to before he was in danger, will he know what's going on when we show up? Second, won't your parents, not to mention the hospital, notice he's gone?"

"I see what you mean," Billy admitted in defeat.

Nik was about to also admit defeat when he was startled by Billy's hand slamming down onto the table.

"I've got it!" Billy shouted. "We'll use the watch to go back to before he was sent to the hospital. We'll get onto the grounds; and then jump forward to the present, find him, and then use the watch to get him out!"

Nik sat speechless for a moment, trying desperately to digest what Billy was saying. After a moment, he began to nod his head in agreement.

"I think that just might work."

"It should," Billy pondered. "We'll have to wait until tomorrow when the sun's out."

Chapter Six

The end of the school day couldn't come quickly enough for Billy and Nik. The final bell sent them dashing out the door and heading toward Billy's house. The sun was still high over the trees, with very little cloud cover to interfere with it. Just perfect, Billy thought. Once they reached the house, they deposited their books in the workshop. After announcing that they were going to the park, they started back toward the center of town. The county hospital was a good hour's walk beyond that. Eventually, they reached their destination; a narrow strip of cleared land just outside the fence that bordered the hospital's grounds. The narrow strip of land was bisected by railroad tracks. They walked along the fence until they were well away from the road, and out of the view of anyone who may be walking the grounds. Billy reached into his pocket and took out the very necessary timepiece. He looked around again to make sure they were not observed.

"Well, here goes," he quipped, flipping the watch open.

"How far back are we going?" Nik asked.

"We should only need to go back a day or two," Billy answered. He turned the stem on the watch, turned it toward the sun, and waited.

To them, it was yesterday. To the rest of the world it was late Sunday afternoon. Billy and Nik were now standing on the hospital side of the fence. They scanned the area to see where they might start looking for Uncle Will. They made their way stealthily across the grounds, coming upon a large metal shed. Peering through a small window, they saw that it housed a large tractor with a mowing deck attached to its rear. As they turned to proceed, they were each seized by the shoulder from behind. The two boys gasped loudly and wheeled around to see Uncle Will grinning at them through his graying beard.

"Took you long enough, didn't it?" he whispered.

"Uncle Will!" Billy hissed. "What are you trying to do, give me a heart attack? How did you get here?"

"Well," the old man replied, "I figured you'd get in here once you got my message. I guess you young fellows have some smarts after all."

As Uncle Will spoke, Billy was studying his face. He noticed that each of Uncle Will's temples bore a small round patch of red skin.

"Uncle Will," he asked, pointing to his own temple, "what happened?"

"Oh, this," Uncle Will smiled. "It's nothing. Let's just say that the good Dr. Janus believes that electroshock therapy is still a viable form of treatment."

Billy and Nik were horrified.

"Mr. Sheppard," Nik asked, "were you...tortured?!"

"Torture," Uncle Will laughed, "is such an ugly word, Nik. The good doctor was merely using an alternative means of persuasion."

"He was trying to get the watch, wasn't he?" Billy assumed. "Who is this guy?"

"I'll tell you later," Uncle Will replied. "Right now, let's blow this joint." He gestured toward the watch in Billy's hand. "May I?"

"Please do," Billy said, handing it to his uncle.

Soon, the boys and Uncle Will were back in the workshop, having made their way back to the house and into the basement without being noticed. Uncle Will promptly made himself comfortable, sitting at the table and leaning back in the chair. His eyes moved across the entire room.

"Cleaned it up a bit, I see," he remarked.

Billy and Nik took two of the remaining chairs and sat down across the table from him.

"Uncle Will," Billy began, "I've got a lot of questions. First off, what's going on with this Dr. Janus? Why does he want the watch? Where did he come from anyway? And why did you give it to me in the first place?"

Uncle Will threw his hands up in mock defeat.

"Whoa, hold on a minute! One question at a time, please. I was just about to tell you everything."

"We're all ears, Uncle Will."

Uncle Will put his feet up on the table, drawing in a long breath.

"I don't think I need to tell you that what I'm about to say does not leave this room. It all started some years ago, before you were born. I was part of a group of men of various backgrounds. We called ourselves The Guild. It was sort of a secret society, the kind of thing that conspiracy theorists like to blame for all the world's problems. Such groups are usually suspected of controlling events from behind the scenes, fixing elections, deposing heads of state, running the economy, things like that. We weren't like that at all, really. We were mainly concerned with protecting and preserving history; making sure things were recorded the way they happened. Only occasionally were we successful."

"So what does the watch have to do with this?" asked Billy.

"This watch," Uncle Will continued, "is one of four that the Guild had possession of, all with the capability to travel through time. The members of the Guild used the watches to travel through time only for the purpose of observation. We were all bound by an oath never to interfere with recorded history. That's why there were more members than watches. That's also why we always kept the watches separated and never allowed more than two members to use them at the same time in the same place."

"Okay, Uncle Will," Billy said, "so this 'Guild' was basically a bunch of guys who used to travel through time to study history and make sure things really happened the way people said they happened, right?"

"Something like that."

"Who started this 'Guild?' asked Nik.

Uncle Will shifted his posture.

"I'm not sure. All I can tell you is what a member of the Guild named Rupert Gould told me. In the early eighteenth century, a man named John Harrison designed a timepiece that was, for its time, revolutionary. It was made to aid navigation at sea. The British government was offering a fortune to anyone who could build an accurate timepiece that could travel by ship, something unheard of in those days. Harrison pulled it off, but the academic establishment basically stonewalled him. He didn't collect the reward until he was in his eighties, too old to do anything with it."

"That stinks," Billy said, "So, this Harrison guy made the watches?"

"Not exactly," Uncle Will continued. "He made some clocks and such, but they were for traveling across oceans, not time. All the while this was going on, his son William Harrison had learned the craft and became his father's apprentice. Now, here's where it gets murky."

The boys unconsciously slid to the edges of their chairs.

"Now, according to historical accounts, William Harrison dropped out of the watch making craft. But then a rumor started to circulate that he was secretly continuing work on another timepiece based on one of his father's later designs. Rupert had an idea that this new design was the one that all the Guild watches were based on. We could only speculate why he would try to design such a thing. Perhaps he was trying to salvage his father's legacy. Maybe it drove him nuts to think that his father could have done so much more if he only had more time." Uncle Will sighed. "The trail pretty much went cold at that point. The Guild could find no evidence. Rupert started researching John Harrison's work, hoping to find clues, but..."

With that, Uncle Will shrugged, and then drummed his fingers on the table.

"So how does Dr. Janus figure into all this?" Billy asked.

Uncle Will paused a moment to collect his thoughts.

"Dr. Alexander Janus was a member of the Guild. He and another member named Roland Peters began to entertain the notion of using the power we had to not merely observe history, but to alter it. After trying to persuade them against such foolishness, the rest of the

Guild tried to find a way to expel them. Once he realized this, Janus disappeared, apparently taking one of the watches with him."

"So why not simply take the watch back?" Nik asked. "We know where he is."

"It's not that easy, Nik," explained Uncle Will. "He's taken into account that the Guild may try to find him; so he's taken steps to prevent that. That partially explains my being institutionalized."

"So, he's basically trying to stop the Guild from finding him," Billy said. "Why not just keep a low profile?"

"Because, Billy," Uncle Will replied, "He's not simply content with the one watch he has; he wants to make sure he's the only one with the power to travel through time. That way, he can change, or control, history, and in so doing, control the future as well. The Guild has, for the last century or so, been trying to fix the damage he's done."

"Damage?" Billy and Nik asked simultaneously.

"Let's just say that all those conspiracy theorists aren't entirely mistaken," Uncle Will said with an acerbic grin.

Billy asked, "Couldn't you travel into the future to see where he is and then head him off?"

"Impossible," was the reply. Uncle Will continued, "The watches cannot travel any further in time than right now."

"I do not understand," Nik said.

Uncle Will got up and approached a small chalkboard that hung over the workbench. With a piece of chalk, he drew a horizontal line from left to right, drawing an arrowhead on the right end. He then drew a number of small hash marks along the line. He drew a larger mark over the arrowhead and labeled it 'Now." He turned and explained.

"Time basically passes in a linear fashion, sort of like tape through a tape recorder. The future hasn't happened yet, so there's nowhere to travel yet. Right now is now. Ten seconds from now, now will be in the past. The farthest forward we can go is...now."

The boys looked like deer hypnotized by headlights. He continued.

"Trust me, boys. We can't travel into the future."

The old man leaned forward and placed his hands on the table, putting his face mere inches from those of the two boys.

"The bottom line is that he won't stop until the rest of the watches are in his possession or destroyed. I had a feeling he'd get this close to me, so I gave the watch to you, Billy. I figured he'd never suspect I'd entrust it to a kid."

"Thanks a lot," Billy smirked.

"Nothing personal," was the reply. "I know you better than that."

"So what must we do?" Nik asked nervously.

"What we must do," Uncle Will began, "is try to find the remaining members of the Guild. Hopefully, we'll be able to find the other watches before Janus does. It won't be easy. The members were not only from different backgrounds, they were from different time periods as well. And no one member knows which other member had a watch."

"So where do we start?" Billy asked. "We can't just go hopping through time looking like we do." He flipped a long lock of hair out of his face. "The last time we tried that, we stuck out like a sore thumb."

"Ah, yes!" Uncle Will exclaimed. "I have a solution to that problem."

With that, turned and made his way to a large circuit breaker panel in the corner. Opening the thin metal door, he flipped a breaker switch located at the bottom of a column of circuit breakers. His action was immediately followed by a muffled, metallic, grinding noise emanating from inside the large steel cabinet that stood against the back wall. Billy and Nik wheeled around in their seats, turning their attention to the sound. Uncle Will approached the cabinet and threw open the doors. To the boys' shock, the back of the cabinet had disappeared, leaving a dark hollow space lined with concrete. From the top of this space hung a single bare light bulb with a short chain. When Uncle Will turned on the light, the boys could see that the space was actually a shaft that extended downward. The back of the shaft had a heavy iron ladder bolted to it.

Uncle Will gestured for the boys to follow him as he grabbed the ladder. They reluctantly poked their heads into the cabinet to see that the shaft extended about thirty feet straight down. At the bottom, they could see another opening. Slowly, they followed Uncle Will down the shaft. Once he reached the bottom, Uncle Will disappeared into the dark doorway. Barely a second later, light poured from the opening. Uncle Will reappeared at the bottom of the shaft.

"Come on, boys," he beckoned, "get the lead out!"

When they reached the doorway at the base of the shaft, the boys were rendered breathless by what they saw. Beyond the doorway was a room that extended back about fifty feet; and it was nearly as wide. The walls were lined with clothing racks, similar to the type one would see in a department store. At different intervals, small placards protruded from between the plastic covered garments. The one closest to the door read: '1750-1760,' the next one, several feet away, read: '1760-1780,' and so on all the way around the room. Nearly every time period for two centuries was represented. There were formal garments and working clothes, even women's clothing, all in excellent condition.

The center of the room was divided in half by several large wooden cabinets, placed back to back. The cabinets consisted mainly of wide flat drawers, all labeled in the same fashion as the clothes. At the tops of some cabinets were signs that read: 'currency,' 'jewelry,' 'weapons,' and 'documents.' Billy approached a cabinet marked 'currency' and opened a drawer. There inside were neatly displayed paper notes. What set them apart from the money Billy was familiar with, besides the size and color, were the words 'Confederate States of America' emblazoned across the top.

Billy approached a large drawer labeled 'documents.' Inside, he found numerous forms of identification from numerous time periods. Most of the documents had Uncle Will's photograph on them, sometimes in color and sometimes in black and white. There were passports from at least a dozen countries, licenses, ID cards, all bearing the name 'William Sheppard.' There was William Sheppard the lawyer, William Sheppard the truck driver, even William Sheppard the FBI agent. Billy slid the drawer shut with raised eyebrows.

Nik stood holding the uniform of a soldier in the Continental Army, its long blue coat with brass buttons looking as if it were hung there yesterday. Hanging it back up, he crossed the room and removed a suit from another rack. It was a 1970's vintage leisure suit, made of polyester that was a hideous shade of green. He replaced it, sticking out his tongue in disgust. Billy approached his uncle, who stood absently winding the watch.

"Where...how..." he stammered, gesturing wildly at the artifacts around them.

For an answer, Uncle Will simply held out the watch, letting it dangle from its chain. This seemed to settle the matter for his addled nephew.

"So this is why you won't let Mom and Dad sell the house," Billy thought aloud.

"What do we do next?" Nik called from across the room. He was wearing a white dinner jacket with a red silk handkerchief in the breast pocket, standing as if he were posing for a fashion magazine. "The name's Brenitski, Nikolai Brenitski."

The other two looked at him, then at each other. Suddenly, all three burst into laughter.

"What we do next," Uncle Will answered, "is start by finding the other members of the Guild to see if and when our friend has called on them. We might be able to locate the remaining watches as well."

"That shouldn't be too hard," said Billy. "We've already got one; we can assume that Dr. Janus has at least one other one. That leaves just two."

"Assuming he hasn't already found them," Nik interjected.

"Yes," Uncle Will agreed, "we should consider that, but we still need to cover all bases."

"So where to?" Billy asked. "Or should I say 'when to?'"

"Back to visit an old friend of mine," said Uncle Will. He approached the clothing rack marked '1760-1780.' "He was a good-standing member of the Guild, as well as a trusted friend."

Uncle Will took three suits of clothes from the rack, all of them typical of the upper class American colonist of the period. Shortly, the three had changed into their costumes, the two boys itching from the coarse fabrics and stiff collars. Their longish hair was tied into ponytails with pieces of dark ribbon. Uncle Will had on a white powdered wig and long frock coat.

"Nice legs," Billy chuckled, pointing to the white silk stockings Nik was wearing. Nik responded with a grimace as he adjusted his three-cornered hat. They hardly noticed that Uncle Will had already climbed back up to the workshop.

"Come on, boys," he called down the shaft, "we're losing sunlight!"

They raced up the ladder to find Uncle Will at the table, typing on a small, palm-sized computer.

"What's that?" asked Billy.

"It's just a small computer I've built for calculating orbital displacement. I just put in our coordinates, then the time we want to travel to. It looks like we'll arrive in the spring of 1776, somewhere on the northeast coast of America. We should find our friend right where I expect him to be."

With that, Uncle Will closed the computer, placed it inside his jacket, and approached the small window at the end of the workshop. He took the watch from his pocket and opened it toward the sunlight streaming in through the window. Soon, the large black hole appeared. Its appearance still startled the boys.

"I just hope we don't end up in hostile Indian Territory," Uncle Will quipped as he stepped through it.

"What?!" the two boys gasped simultaneously, just as they passed through the hole behind him.

Chapter Seven

"Just kidding!" Uncle Will laughed.

The sun was shining on the wide dirt road leading out of Trenton, New Jersey. Uncle Will and the boys had, thankfully, not ended up in Indian Territory. Indians had not lived in this part of the country for quite some time. Billy had a hard time believing that, because the road seemed to wind off into nothing but thick woods. There were no visible signs of what he considered to be civilization. It took several minutes for Uncle Will to convince the two boys that he knew exactly where he was going. They made their way on foot toward the Delaware River, where Uncle Will hired a boatman to take them across the river to Pennsylvania. There, they proceeded southward, coming upon a horse and rider. The horseman tipped his hat and smiled as he passed. For a moment, Billy thought he had seen the man somewhere before. He looked over his shoulder to see the rider goad the horse from a slow trot to a gallop, disappearing around a bend in the road. Billy dismissed the notion that the rider was familiar to him.

"Where are we headed, anyway?" he asked his uncle.

"Philadelphia," Uncle Will replied. "My friend should be there."

After a few hours of walking, with regular stops to rest, the group reached Philadelphia late in the afternoon. The streets were alive with activity. Dust filled the air as a team of horses pulled a large wagon along the crowded street. Uncle Will walked purposefully along the street, as easily as he would have if he were back in Cannon Falls. Billy and Nik did as best they could to keep up with him; but it was difficult when there was so much that was strange about their surroundings. As the three of them passed a large open grassy area, they observed a group of young men performing what appeared to be military drills. They soon made their way to the center of town, where they came upon a large brick building with a large bell tower extending from the top of the facade. Uncle Will led them to a shade tree across the square from the building and sat on the ground. The boys did likewise.

"Are we going to meet your friend here?" asked Nik.

"He should be coming out of that building soon enough," Uncle

Will answered.

"Uncle Will," Billy asked, "isn't that Independence Hall?" He had recalled pictures of it in history class.

"Not at this point in time," Uncle Will said. "For now, it's just the Pennsylvania state house."

At that moment, a group of men was coming out of the building, congregating on the steps. One of the men was a stocky fellow with long, stringy hair and spectacles. He began to walk down the steps when Uncle Will arose and waved to him. The two boys sat gaping as they recognized him.

"Ben!" Uncle Will called. "Ben Franklin!"

"Mr. Sheppard," Franklin answered with an enthusiastic wave, "this is indeed a surprise. How are you?"

The two met and heartily shook hands.

"How are things going?" Uncle Will asked, gesturing toward the state house.

"Ah," replied Franklin with a heavy sigh, "the document is finally starting to take form. It won't be long now." He looked over the top of his spectacles at the two boys, who by now had clamored to their feet. Uncle Will introduced them.

"May I present my nephew, Master William Maxwell, and our friend, Master Nikolai Brenitski."

"The pleasure is all mine," Franklin said, nodding toward them. The boys continued to gape inanely.

"You'll have to excuse them, Ben," explained Uncle Will. "They're great admirers of yours."

"Admirers!" Franklin raised his eyebrows. "I'm honored. Gentlemen, I would be further honored if you would join me at my home for dinner."

"We accept," Uncle Will responded.

The group headed in the direction of Franklin's home, with the old statesman leading the way. As they walked, Billy took his uncle aside.

"Uncle Will," he whispered, "what was the document he was talking about before?"

"The Declaration of Independence. Don't they teach you kids anything in school?"

"Wow!"

Eventually, they arrived at Franklin's home. It was simple and typical of the period. The rooms were small and the corridors narrow. A comfortable summer breeze coursed through the open windows. The furnishings were also simple. A black wrought iron stove stood as the centerpiece of the sitting room. As Billy's eyes moved over the room, he noticed something barely visible in the corner behind a large desk. He craned his neck to see a small cloth kite leaning against the wall. It looked just like any other kite, except for a charred hole in the cloth about the size of a man's fist. Billy suppressed a chuckle.

Shortly thereafter, dinner was served. Billy and Nik stiffly forced down the meal of veal and corn, trying to maintain their composure. They were not prepared for the lack of preservatives, artificial flavoring, and other chemicals in what was set before them. Nik spent more time shooing flies away from his plate than eating off it. Uncle Will ate contentedly, chatting with Franklin. At one point, Billy discretely leaned toward his uncle to ask him to identify another piece of meat on his plate.

"It's neck of mutton," Uncle Will whispered.

"Neck of what?"

"Just shut up and eat it."

Billy sighed and stabbed at it with his fork.

Uncle Will turned to Franklin. "You do look well, Ben."

"As do you," Franklin replied.

"Ben, I'd like to say that this is a social call," Uncle Will said, his expression turning serious, "but I'm afraid that's not the case."

"What's on your mind, Will?"

"It's about the Guild."

At this, Franklin put his fork down and leaned back in his chair. The heavy silence that followed compelled the boys to awkwardly do likewise. Uncle Will continued.

"It seems our friend Dr. Janus is attempting to acquire all the watches. He still has Peters working with him."

"Yes, I know," Franklin interrupted. "Peters paid a call on me some days ago."

"Looking for one of the watches?"

"Yes; and I'll tell you what I told him." Franklin started to look somewhat angry. "When Janus allowed himself to become as corrupt as we swore we never would, I knew it was only a matter of time - you'll pardon my pun - until the whole Guild would be dragged down with him, or be wasted in trying to thwart him. It would seem the latter is true."

"Quite," replied Uncle Will.

"And as far as the watches are concerned," Franklin continued, thumping his index finger on the table, "I don't have one, and I don't want one!"

"Mr. Franklin," Billy asked, "you were a member of the Guild?"

"I was," said Franklin with a smile. "I see your uncle has expanded the membership somewhat. I always said that three men can keep a secret if two of them are dead."

Billy immediately recalled the first time he heard that. He gave a puzzled glance to Uncle Will, who responded with a wink.

"I had to, Ben," Uncle Will said. "Janus almost acquired this one." He held out the large gold watch. Franklin gently cradled it in his hand.

"Ah, Tempus Fugit. Who else have you accounted for?"

"So far," replied Uncle Will, "we've accounted for you and me. Oh, and Rupert Gould."

"Rupert? Does he have one? How goes his work on those other pieces you told me about?"

"Unfortunately, he doesn't have a watch - of any kind."

Franklin was taken aback. "What do you mean?"

Uncle Will explained, "The last I heard, Rupert had suffered a nervous breakdown in the middle of his research. It had already cost him his marriage. He is now confined to an asylum. They took away whatever timepieces he may have had, blaming his obsession with them for his condition."

"I am very sorry to hear such news. That leaves James and Marcus then, doesn't it?" asked Franklin.

"It would seem so."

Franklin's mood shifted. "Tell me, Will, are they still going to use that ghastly portrait of me for their currency where you're from? Or should I say 'when?'"

Billy and Nik stopped and stared in amazement as Uncle Will responded with a chuckle.

"Yes, I'm afraid so. What's more, their going to redesign the note to make the picture larger."

"God save us all!" Franklin exclaimed in mock despair. He then rose from the table.

"Gentlemen, I shall now make arrangements for you to stay the night. I assume you'll want to be on your way with the first sunlight."

Billy asked, "We're going to spend the night here? Our parents don't even know where we are!"

"Not a problem," Uncle Will said. "They don't even know you're gone. We'll return to Cannon Falls at the exact moment in time that we left. It will be as if we didn't leave in the first place."

Chapter Eight

With the coming of daylight, the group returned to Uncle Will's workshop, at the exact minute they had left, just as he had explained.

"Omigosh, omigosh," Billy sputtered, pacing back and forth.

"That was Benjamin Franklin!" Nik gasped. "Billy, THAT WAS BENJAMIN FRANKLIN!"

The boys continued to mutter and pace as Uncle Will leaned against the workbench, looking quite pleased with himself.

"Gentlemen," he said, trying to bring them back to earth, "I appreciate your excitement, but we still have a lot of work to do." He removed his jacket and began to unbutton his embroidered waistcoat. Billy sat down and removed the black leather shoes that were beginning to make his feet sore. As he looked up at his uncle, who by now was removing his shirt, he noticed a faint red mark on the inside of Uncle Will's elbow. It closely resembled a hypodermic needle mark. He paused, wondering what to make of it. He decided not to bring it up for the moment.

"What was all that about that Rupert fellow? Why did he have a nervous breakdown?"

"Rupert was in the process of reconstructing the original John Harrison clocks," Uncle Will explained. "In the middle of his work, World War II started, and the clocks were moved and put in storage. His wife had already left him, so I guess that sort of pushed him over the edge. It's a shame, really. Heck of a nice guy. I have to wonder how close he was to finding something, and whether or not Janus knew what he was up to. It's a safe bet he's pretty much out of the picture for now."

"So we just need to find two more members, right?" asked Nik.

"It's a start. James Maybrick and Marcus Straker. I knew them both pretty well."

"Who do we look for first?" Billy asked.

"Well, I suppose Marcus would be easy to find," Uncle Will responded. "The last time I heard news of him, he too had been committed to an insane asylum. Now, I wouldn't doubt it if Janus was behind that."

"I'm starting to see a pattern here, myself," said Billy, half under his breath.

Uncle Will responded with a loud belly laugh. The two boys smiled uneasily at him, glancing at each other in apprehension.

"It's completely understandable, boys," the old man said, "When you've got the power to change events that the world could do without, and you have to refuse. Well, that could drive a guy nuts!"

"I guess it would," replied Billy.

"So, where should we go next?" Nik asked. "Or should I say 'when?'"

"To answer your second question," Uncle Will began, "we'll remain in the present for now. As to 'where,' you two need to go downtown to get haircuts."

"Haircuts?!" the boys reacted in near horror.

"Haircuts. Where we're going, long hair on young men is frowned upon. Too bad it's not frowned upon here."

"But...," Billy began to protest.

"But nothing, boy."

It was agreed that Billy and Nik would go downtown to get haircuts, while Uncle Will would stay hidden in the basement. Barely an hour later, when they returned, the boys passed through the kitchen on the way to the basement. Carolyn was at the counter, slicing vegetables.

"Billy!" she exclaimed. "Did you actually get a hair cut?!" She put down her knife and ran her hand across the back of Billy's head. He had no choice but to stand there and take it.

"Uh, yeah."

"Well, what possessed you to do this?"

Billy stood glancing at Nik out the corner of his eye, grasping for an answer.

"Uh...," Billy attempted, "uh...I just wanted to try a new look."

"Mm hmm," Carolyn smiled. "Your father should be happy to see it."

"Well," replied Billy, "we're just going down to the workshop for a while."

The pair wasted not another second returning to the basement to find Uncle Will sitting at the table, wearing a three-piece suit with a stiff white collar. In his lap, he held a bowler hat.

"Much better," he said. "Now, if you'll get changed, we can get going." He gestured to two similar outfits hanging from the tool cabinet door.

"Where to?" asked Billy as he got dressed.

"1915," Uncle Will responded, handing the watch to Billy.

"Don't we need to calculate for orbital drift?" Nik asked.

"I already have. I've gone back to 1915 quite often."

"What for?"

"You'll see."

Soon, they were all properly dressed and ready to go. Billy snapped the watch open.

It was cloudy when they arrived in Leeds, England. Uncle Will informed the boys of where they were and began to lead them down a remote gravel road. The green hills extended as far as the eye could see in all directions. The relative silence was broken by the occasional passage of an automobile. Eventually, they reached the center of town, where there stood a train station. People were filing in and out of the building, as the sounds of a steam locomotive could be heard. Uncle Will led the boys inside the terminal and instructed them to wait near a large pillar. He made his way to a ticket window.

"I need passage for three to Victoria Station, London."

After paying for the tickets, he collected the boys; and the three entered the platform to wait for their train.

"What's in London?" Billy asked with a hint of impatience. His feet were aching from the long walk to the station.

"Queen Mary," Uncle Will answered matter-of-factly.

"Yeah, right," Billy retorted, ribbing Nik with his elbow.

Billy would soon be amazed at how serious his uncle was. By late afternoon, the three had arrived at Buckingham Palace. They were just in time for a formal reception of some kind, as evidenced by the steady stream of well-dressed people walking through the gate, some in military uniforms. Billy and Nik were amazed at how Uncle Will seemed to know exactly where to go, as if he were again completely familiar with his surroundings. When he approached the gate, he took a small card from his pocket and showed it to the guard who was busily admitting the guests. The guard immediately nodded and motioned for another guard standing nearby. He showed the card to the second guard, who then waved Uncle Will through the gate, followed by the two boys.

As they followed Uncle Will around the hall, they were equally amazed at how many of those present knew him. He shook hands heartily with the gentlemen and kissed the hands of every lady he met. What happened next stopped them dead in their tracks. A tall, dark haired, beautiful woman in a flowing, white ball gown greeted them. She practically sparkled from head to toe with every kind of jewel. Her hair was framed by a diamond tiara that shone in the candlelight.

"William!" She almost sang the name.

"Your majesty," Uncle Will responded with a bow. He took the gloved hand she extended to him and kissed it gently.

"It's so good to see you again," she said shyly, her eyes sparkling like the jewels she wore. "You look tired, William. Are you well?"

"Yes, I'm quite well," he replied, rising to his full height. "I've just been doing a bit of traveling."

Billy and Nik glanced at each other behind his back.

"You brought some friends," the woman said, gesturing to the boys.

"Your majesty, may I present my nephew, William Maxwell, and our friend, Nikolai Brenitski." Uncle Will stepped aside as she approached the boys. They bowed almost instinctively, as if compelled by her presence. She placed her gloved hand before Billy. He followed his uncle's cue and took it and kissed it, his own hand shaking nervously. He looked up at her smiling face, still clutching her hand.

"Uh, Billy," Uncle Will whispered, leaning toward him, "she's going to want that hand back."

His uncle's voice snapped him to attention, and he released her hand, apologizing profusely. She proceeded to Nik, who was still bent low, his eyes directed at the floor. He kissed her hand shyly and stepped back.

"Gentlemen," Uncle Will said, "may I present Her Royal Majesty, Queen Mary."

The boys stood speechless. The awkward silence was broken by a booming voice from behind them.

"I remember well the days when she had that same effect on me."

They turned to see a tall man with neatly groomed hair, a short beard, and a large bushy mustache. He was dressed in full military regalia, a shining sword hanging from his belt, the polished brass buttons of his coat reflecting the light.

"George," said Mary, approaching him and placing her arm around his. Uncle Will and the boys bowed again as introductions were made.

"William," King George asked Uncle Will, "what brings you to London again?"

"I'm looking up an old friend, Your Highness." Uncle Will paused. "I'm looking for Marcus Straker."

The mention of that name brought a marked change in the king's expression.

"There's a name I haven't heard in quite a while."

"You knew him, your highness?" Billy asked.

"I knew him well," the king replied. "A genius of a man. One of the most honorable and compassionate human beings one could have the pleasure of knowing. What a shame."

"Indeed," Uncle Will interjected. "I understand he's gone quite insane."

"He has," King George continued. "You can find him in the Briarcliff Sanitarium. I don't know if he can take visitors, though."

"I guess I'll find out," said Uncle Will.

That was followed by another awkward silence, which was soon broken by Queen Mary.

"Nikolai, I gather from your name that you are Russian."

"Yes, I am."

"Then you'll want to meet my cousin, Empress Alexandra."

Nik had to think for a moment to remember why that name

sounded familiar. Quickly, he recalled his history lessons in Russia and realized that the queen was referring to the Tsaritsa.

"She's here?!"

"She is," the queen continued. "She's right over there." When they looked toward where she pointed, they noticed a dark-haired woman with a rather serious expression, in a white, floor length dress. She was attended by a small number of servants. Billy looked at Nik in pleasant surprise.

"Well," Uncle Will said, "we don't wish to keep you from your guests. Come on, boys, let's mingle."

Before long, Uncle Will was off, conversing with other dignitaries, leaving the boys to wander aimlessly throughout the hall. As they took in the atmosphere, they found themselves glancing repeatedly at a young girl across the room. She seemed about their age, with long, blondish hair and blue eyes. She was wearing a simple, ivory colored dress. On more than one occasion, her eyes met with theirs, and she would smile shyly, then look away.

"Billy, do you see that girl over there?" Nik asked.

"The one you've been staring at for the last ten minutes?"

"You're one to talk!"

"What about her?"

"She's beautiful."

"So why don't you go talk to her?"

Nik looked at Billy for a moment, mulling over his suggestion. Before Billy could respond further, Nik was weaving through the crowd toward her, with Billy in hot pursuit. As they drew near, she turned away from the group she was standing with and looked squarely at them. The boys stopped cold, unsure of what to do next.

"You didn't look like you were having much fun," Nik said, his Russian accent thickening with anxiety, "so I thought..."

"We thought," Billy interrupted.

"Uh...WE thought we'd come over and say 'hello.'" Nik turned and looked daggers at Billy.

She responded with a smile, and much to their surprise, answered in Russian. Nik, pleased at this turn of events, began to converse with her, leaving Billy completely in the dark.

"Uh...Nik," Billy said, "what are you guys saying?"

"I was just telling him," her response in stilted English surprised them again, "that I am so glad to meet someone here who speaks Russian."

"Hey," Billy said, raising his eyebrows, "is your mother, by any chance, Empress Alexandra?"

The girl nodded in response. Just then, the Empress herself approached with Queen Mary by her side.

"Ah, boys," said the queen, "I see you've met Grand Duchess Anastasia."

Chapter Nine

"Can you believe those two?" Billy smirked. He lifted a porcelain teacup to his lips.

"They sure seem to have hit it off," Uncle Will replied with a hint if consternation.

"Yeah, and I saw her first," remarked Billy bluntly.

He and Uncle Will were sitting at a small round table on the sunlit patio, not far from the palace. A few tables away, Nik and Anastasia sat talking in Russian. Occasionally, Nik would glance over at Uncle Will, remembering the "briefing" of sorts they had about conversing with her. He was instructed not to discuss anything that would reveal what to her would be the future, as it could result in quite a shock. This meant saying nothing about the Soviet Union, the Russian Revolution of 1917, and certainly nothing about the murder of the Romanov family at the hands of the Bolsheviks.

"It's a shame, really," said Uncle Will, stirring his coffee.

"What is?"

"That such a lovely young girl should meet such a horrible end."

"And there's nothing we can do?"

"To do anything about it would be to change the course of history."

Billy sighed. "That could drive a guy..."

"Crazy?"

"Yeah." Billy was beginning to understand more and more why everyone thought his uncle was not quite right. He glanced across the patio to Anastasia. She smiled at him furtively, and then quickly looked downward.

"What are we doing today?" asked Billy.

"Today," Uncle Will replied, "we go to Briarcliff Sanitarium to look in on our friend Marcus."

Uncle Will rose from the table. Billy followed him to the other table.

"We need to get going, Nik," Uncle Will said. "I want you to stay with the Grand Duchess here at the palace and wait for us. We shouldn't be long."

Nik enthusiastically agreed to do so, a little too enthusiastically for Billy's comfort. Billy and his uncle headed for the sanitarium.

Within a half an hour, they were entering the building, a dreary looking stone structure with overgrown shrubbery clogging its facade. It was much darker and seemed more foreboding than the county hospital where Uncle Will had been. Inside, the gray plaster walls and hardwood floors echoed every sound. Uncle Will approached the heavy wooden desk that stood between the entrance and a long dark corridor. Seated at the desk was a large woman in a starched white nurse's uniform. She eyed the two of them suspiciously.

"Can I 'elp you?" she asked with a Cockney accent.

"I'm here to see one Marcus Straker."

"Wait 'ere."

The nurse rose to her six-foot height and disappeared down the corridor. As Billy and Uncle Will waited, Billy found himself rather distracted by the distant noises that seemed to come from all directions. The sounds had echoed off the walls of the corridor to the point of being indistinguishable. He required a nudge from Uncle Will when the woman reappeared a moment later.

"Follow me."

They did as instructed, passing down the long hallway, which seemed to get darker and more cavernous with each step. Along the way stood heavy muscular attendants, carrying large iron rings filled with keys. There were also several patients, some simply standing and staring coldly into space, others shouting at each other in incoherent tones. The dismal atmosphere was suddenly broken when, from out of a darkened side hallway, a man darted into the main corridor. He was totally naked except for a pair of tattered socks that caused him to skid wildly out of control. This allowed the two minders who pursued him to catch up and detain him. As they tried to hold him down, a steady stream of obscenities issued from his mouth. Billy stood there mortified until his uncle took him by the arm and led him on. The nurse turned a corner at the end of the corridor and stopped in front of a heavy wooden door. She gestured to a man standing nearby to come and unlock the door.

"You 'ave ten minutes," she said coldly, walking past Billy and his uncle without looking at them. The attendant, a short, plump man with bulbous eyes, unlocked the door and put his head slowly into the room.

"Mr. Straker," he cooed, "you 'ave guests." He turned to Uncle Will. "I doubt if 'e'll even acknowledge you."

The man stepped aside to admit the two into the room. It was about ten feet square, with pale colored walls that showed traces of mildew. A musty smell hung in the still air. The barely adequate single lightbulb fixed into the ceiling cast cold shadows everywhere. In one corner was a narrow cot covered with an assortment of frayed and tattered blankets. As their eyes scanned the room, they saw stacks of books randomly piled about the floor. Marcus Straker was sitting on the bed scribbling feverishly in a book. He was a short, frail, balding man with gray eyes and gray hair, which stuck out in all directions. His skin was ashen and wrinkled, except for a bright red patch on the inside of his forearm, which was punctuated by obvious needle marks. He was dressed in white pajamas that bore unidentifiable stains. He did not look up from his writing.

"A diller, a dollar, a ten o'clock scholar. And what makes you come so soon?" he said with a loud, cracking voice. "You used to come at ten o'clock, but now you come at noon!"

"Marcus," Uncle Will said carefully, "it's me, William."

"A diller, a dollar, a diller, a dollar," was the reply.

Billy began to look at the books all around him. He noticed, from the titles on their spines, that they were all history books, as was the book in which Marcus scribbled. As he continued to study the room, Uncle Will sat on the bed next to Marcus.

"Marcus, it's about the Guild. I need to know..."

"They've got it all wrong, all wrong!" Marcus shouted, holding his book in front of Uncle Will's face. Uncle Will took the book and looked at it. Raising his eyebrows, he handed it to Billy. Billy flipped through the pages, observing that whole paragraphs were scribbled over and replaced with passages written in the margins. Marcus seemed to be rewriting the text, making "corrections" to the history recorded there.

"Marcus," Uncle Will was starting to sound impatient, "I need to know if you had one of the watches. Has Janus been here?"

With that, Marcus reared up and sat on his haunches in the middle of the bed. He began to rock back and forth slowly, scratching at the needle marks in his arm.

"A diller, a dollar, a ten o'clock scholar. And what makes you come so soon? You used to come at ten o'clock, but now you come at noon!" Now the rhyme was a rapid mumble.

Uncle Will stood in front of Marcus, placing his hands on Marcus' shoulders. Suddenly, a tap on his own shoulder interrupted him. He turned to see Billy holding a small wooden box with an open top.

"This might answer your question," said Billy with a heavy sigh. "I found it under the bed."

Inside the box were the remains of a pocket watch. The clock-works, what was left of them, were loosely scattered around a dented gold case, its barely intact hinge allowing the cover to flap open when a horrified Uncle Will lifted it out of the box. Every time the box was moved, gears and pinions would noisily slide around inside. The glass over the face of the watch was shattered, partially exposing the bent hands. Inside the lid was a bare, pitted metal surface. Uncle Will closed the cover to reveal the inscription on the front:

"Tempus Omnia Vulneres Coalescet"

"What does that mean?" asked Billy, looking over his uncle's shoulder.

"Time heals all wounds," Uncle Will said softly. "All wounds except for its own, apparently."

He placed the smashed watch back in the box and slid it under the bed. He looked back at Marcus, who was still rocking slowly; his head turned to the side, like a naughty child waiting to be punished.

"They've got it all wrong, all wrong," he muttered as tears began to well up in his eyes.

"I know, Marcus," Uncle Will whispered as he helped the man over onto his side.

"I'm tired," Marcus sobbed, clutching Uncle Will's hand, "so tired. I want to go back."

"It's all right," replied Uncle Will. As Marcus' head touched the pillow, he turned over to face the wall, and curled into a fetal position, still weeping. Uncle Will gently placed one of the ragged blankets over him. He then crossed the room slowly and tapped on the door, which was immediately opened by the attendant. As he followed his uncle out, Billy thought he saw Uncle Will wipe a tear from his eye.

Billy and his uncle met Nik and Anastasia at the fountain in front of Buckingham Palace. It was just as well, because earlier that day, they had accepted an invitation by the king and queen to have lunch in the palace, so they joined the other guests in a large drawing room. Uncle Will sat pensively in a small armchair, looking out the window. Billy, Nik, and Anastasia strolled around the room, admiring the decor. Anastasia cradled a Kodak "Brownie" camera under one arm. Coming to a large window, she gestured to the boys to stand near it as she lifted her camera to her eye. They did so, putting their arms around each other's shoulder, and she snapped the picture.

"Thank you, both of you, for everything," she said with a Russian accent. "I had such a wonderful time."

The boys each smiled modestly and nodded.

"Perhaps you could come to visit us at the Alexander Palace."

"Well," Billy replied, "if we're in that neck of the woods..."

"I wish we could stay longer, but we are leaving after lunch."

She sat on the end of a sofa, placing her camera on a nearby table. The rest of the afternoon was spent enjoying a rather large meal of every imaginable type of food, at least as far as Billy or Nik had ever seen. It was more like Thanksgiving dinner than lunch to them, much better than the fare at Ben Franklin's home. Afterwards, the guests returned to the drawing room to mingle before they departed one small group at a time. Eventually, it was time for Anastasia and her family to leave. She allowed the boys to escort her to the waiting car that would take her to the Tsar's yacht, *Standart*, and then home to Russia. When they reached the vehicle, she thanked them again for their company, gently shaking their hands. They stood, waving sheepishly, as the car drove off.

"Come on boys," Uncle Will called to them from the gate, "we've got places to go and people to see."

The boys reluctantly made their way back inside. Uncle Will led them to a small anteroom.

"Where are we headed now?" asked Billy.

"Back to the workshop to change our clothes," Uncle Will answered. "Oh, by the way, you should be interested in this."

With that, Uncle Will handed Billy a small, box-like object.

"Anastasia's camera!" both boys exclaimed.

"She must have forgotten it." Uncle Will explained. "We'll take it back with us. There's no way we'll catch up with her now."

Before long, Uncle Will and the two boys were back in the workshop. Billy carefully placed the camera on the workbench and turned to see his uncle slip down the shaft to the vault. He leaned into the steel cabinet to call down to him.

"Where, and when, are we headed now? "

"We need to go back to September, 1889," Uncle Will said. "I've already made the necessary calculations."

"What's back then?" asked Billy.

"You'll see."

Chapter Ten

When they arrived, the remnant of a light fog still hung in the air. They had arrived just before sunrise. The chill in the air was evident in the small clouds that appeared each time they exhaled. Uncle Will drew in a long, deep breath, closed his eyes, and grinned contentedly. Billy and Nik scanned the unfamiliar hills and trees, trying to find their bearings. A thin slice of sunlight was beginning to appear on the horizon.

"It's so good to be back," said Uncle Will.

"Back where?" Billy asked.

"Home!"

Billy and Nik looked at each other, befuddled, as Uncle Will began to stroll up the hill. The boys shrugged and followed him, his brisk gait causing them to lag several paces behind.

"What's he talking about?" Nik whispered to Billy. "Has he ever lived here?"

"Not that I know of," replied Billy, whirling an index finger next to his head.

Uncle Will stopped at the crest of the hill and looked out across a wide, green valley that stretched as far as he could see. The boys caught up with him, trying to catch their breath.

"Where are we going?" Billy asked.

"There." Uncle Will pointed into the valley toward a small clearing. At the center of that stood a large house, still half enshrouded in fog. Before Billy or Nik could focus on it, Uncle Will was bounding down the hill toward the house. They nearly had to sprint to keep up with him. Billy couldn't believe that a man Uncle Will's age could move so fast. Uncle Will cackled with glee as he leapt over rocks and fallen tree branches. When they reached the edge of the clearing, the mansion's full size became evident. Billy and Nik stopped there and watched the last traces of fog peel away from the house.

It stood two stories high, with very tall windows and marble columns across the front of its sand colored stonework. The south end of the building was comprised almost entirely of glass and wrought iron. It looked to Billy like a greenhouse that had been stood on end and attached to the side of the house. A wide gravel footpath circled around the other end of the house.

Suddenly, they heard the sound of barking dogs, coming from one end of the clearing. They turned to see two large Irish wolfhounds running toward Uncle Will, who held his hands out to them. The dogs leapt around him, licking at his hands. He responded by scratching their necks. At that moment, the front door of the house flew open to reveal a tall woman wearing a long, dark, embroidered dress. She had auburn hair, gray eyes, a thin nose, and high cheekbones.

"William!" she shouted, running toward him. Uncle Will was already moving toward her.

"Catherine!" The two met and embraced. She whooped with delight as he lifted her off the ground and spun around. When she touched down, they kissed passionately.

"Oh, William, I could not be happier!" she laughed. She looked over his shoulder and noticed the two boys standing dumbfounded. "One of you must be Billy."

Billy stepped forward and nodded, still looking completely clueless.

"Forgive me," Uncle Will said. "Billy, I'd like you to meet my wife, your Aunt Catherine."

"Your WIFE?!" Billy's jaw dropped. Nik was equally flabbergasted. Uncle Will giggled awkwardly.

"William, I'm surprised at you!" Catherine scolded. She turned to Billy. "He's so absent-minded sometimes." Billy responded with a slow nod, his mouth still hanging open.

"And this is Billy's friend, Nikolai," Uncle Will interrupted.

"Nikolai," Catherine smiled, "what a pleasant surprise."

Nik looked at her with the same open-mouthed stare. She looked back at both boys with a reassuring expression. She seemed to understand completely what a shock they just had.

"Where is Gwyneth?" asked Uncle Will.

"She's in the garden," Catherine answered, pointing toward the side of the house. "Perhaps you could surprise her."

The whole group made its way slowly around to the back of the house. As they did, they were met with the sight of a large, neatly landscaped flower garden. At the center of this sea of colors was a small reflecting pool. A stone footpath led from the patio behind the house out to the garden and around the pool. A young girl was kneeling at the edge of the pool with her hands folded in front of her, her head bowed in prayer. Her long auburn hair was bound up much the same way that Catherine's was. She wore a burgundy dress that extended to her ankles. When she finished praying, she crossed herself and rose to her feet. As she walked around the edge of the pool, the morning sun reflected off a large gold medallion that hung around her neck. Billy and Nik were immediately taken by her gracefulness. She seemed to float as she walked. Only when she reached the entrance to the garden did she notice her admirers. She raised a hand to her mouth as her eyes widened. The boys were puzzled, unsure of why she looked so startled.

"Father!" she blurted out, breaking into a run toward Uncle Will. He caught her in his arms, and she buried her face in his shoulder. It was the boys' turn to look startled. When she finally let go of her father, Gwyneth turned around and apologized profusely for what she called her "unseemly behavior," wiping tears from her gray eyes.

"Gwyneth," her father said, "I'd like you to meet your cousin Billy and his friend Nikolai."

Gwyneth bowed her head slightly and shook hands with them. Billy's mouth hung open again as he grasped for words.

Uncle Will leaned toward him. "You keep your mouth open like that, you'll start catching flies."

Billy caught his composure, snapped his jaw shut, and sneered at Uncle Will.

"Father has told me so much about you," she said, her voice sounding almost musical. Billy was still silent. Uncle Will clapped him on the shoulder.

"Why don't we all go inside and get acquainted?"

Later that day, Gwyneth, Billy, and Nik strolled around the garden in the afternoon sun. She walked between them, her arms intertwined with theirs. The air was heavy with the fragrance of flowers, as well as the sounds of birds. Uncle Will and Aunt Catherine were sitting on two rattan chairs on the patio. A small table stood between them, carrying a pitcher of lemonade. They sipped contentedly from tall glasses.

"I still can't believe that Uncle Will's married," said Billy. "He never told any of us."

"Well," replied Nik, "it would be awfully hard to explain it when your wife was born a hundred years before you were."

"I guess."

"And imagine what it must be like, not being able to tell anyone."

"They'd think he was nuts."

Gwyneth chuckled at this comment.

"What's so funny?" asked Billy.

"Father did say you rescued him from an insane asylum."

"So what else did he tell you?"

"The last time I saw him," Gwyneth began, the smile disappearing from her face, "he told me that a very evil man had a watch just like his, and that he had to stop him from finding the others. He said that he might not come back for a very long time. I asked him if he might not come back at all, and…he said that was…a possibility."

"So you know about the Guild?" asked Nik.

"I know a little about it."

"But you know about Dr. Janus."

"Is that his name?" she responded. "Yes, I know about him. Father told me that he is a very dangerous man. I've been so afraid for my father since he left. I've also been afraid for you, Billy. I've prayed for you often."

"Why me?" Billy's eyebrows shot up.

"Because my father said, before he left, that he may have to give you the watch to keep Dr. Janus from getting it. He said you were the only one he could trust with it. I just hope he can find the others."

Billy stopped and turned to face her. He could see the fear in her eyes.

"Don't worry, Gwyneth. We'll find the watches, and we'll keep an eye on Uncle Will."

She forced a smile in response. "Let's not talk any more of such things today."

The boys heartily agreed, and they continued to escort Gwyneth along the footpath.

"Gwyneth?" Nik asked with a flirtatious grin, "May I ask how old you are?"

"I'm fourteen years old. Why?"

"Don't even think about it," Billy snapped, knowing from experience exactly what Nik was thinking.

"What?" Nik put on an expression of mock defensiveness.

"You know what. She's family. You mess with her, and you'll have me to deal with."

"Billy, Nik, I..." Gwyneth was taking this exchange much too seriously. The look on her face told them that she was thoroughly convinced they were about to come to blows.

"It's okay Gwyneth," Billy assured her. "Watch out for this guy. He's no good for you."

"Thanks," Nik replied sarcastically.

"Besides, what would Anastasia think?" Billy asked with a mocking glimpse at Nik, who responded with a glare.

"Who?" asked Gwyneth.

"A girl we met...some time in the near future," Billy explained. "She's a grand duchess." He said this with an air of pretentiousness.

"I'm flattered," Gwyneth giggled. "I am sure not every young man would favor me over a grand duchess."

With the passing of sunset, the party moved into a large library, just inside from the patio. The room was the entire height of the house, lined from floor to ceiling with bookshelves. A spiral staircase led to a balcony with a wrought iron railing that ran the perimeter of the room, allowing access to the higher shelves. At one point, there was a doorway leading from the balcony to the second floor of the house. At the center of the library was a huge brass globe of the Earth, spanning about four feet across, mounted on a large gimbal that was partially sunk into the floor. The globe itself was fitted with two thin intersecting rings, made up of separate concentric rings. On each of the main rings was a small brass pointer in the shape of a plumb bob. At one end of the gimbal was a metal box with a large crank handle fixed into one side. Three large crystal knobs were set into the top of the box.

A large telescope stood in the corner of the room. This corner of the room was the huge wall of glass that Billy had seen outside earlier. The rest of the furniture in the room was the kind of Victorian furniture that was in Billy's own home. He started to understand how Uncle Will acquired such fine pieces.

The globe especially intrigued Billy. Uncle Will explained its purpose.

"That globe is basically a mechanical version of this." He held up the orbital displacement calculator. "I can use it, along with that telescope, to make the calculations; but it's time consuming. Using the computer is much quicker, and obviously easier to carry."

Billy took a seat on a large sofa next to his cousin, with Nik sitting at the other end. Uncle Will sat in a side chair near the large marble fireplace that adorned one wall. He stabbed at the burning embers with a long, brass poker. Aunt Catherine sat in an armchair working on a cross-stitch.

"What's our plan at this point?" asked Billy.

"Our plan," Uncle Will responded, "is to look for James Maybrick. The last I heard of him, he did not live far from here. The name of the town is Aigburth. It's just south of Liverpool."

"William, dear," Aunt Catherine interrupted, "you have been gone a long time. Mr. Maybrick is dead!"

Her announcement caused all mouths, except for hers and Gwyneth's, in the room to drop open. Uncle Will abruptly rose to his feet.

"Dead?! How?"

"Well this may seem a bit of a shock," she continued, as if her earlier statement was not, "but, it would appear that his wife poisoned him with arsenic. She was tried and sentenced for it not one whole month ago."

"The folks in Liverpool have talked about little else," said Gwyneth.

"Arsenic poisoning? Florie?" Uncle Will half shouted. "That's ridiculous!"

He stood, leaning against the gray marble of the fireplace, trying to collect his thoughts. Billy and Nik looked at each other, trying to gauge what Uncle Will would do next.

"We've got to find her," he finally said. "Where are they holding her?"

"Walton Jail, I think," answered Aunt Catherine.

The following morning, Uncle Will arranged for a coach to transport him and the boys to Liverpool. Once they arrived, they made short work of locating the jail. Uncle Will presented himself to the jailer as an attorney needing to consult with Florie Maybrick, whom the jailer referred to as "Prisoner L.P. 29." The boys followed him inside. The jail looked very much like Briarcliff Sanitarium in its dreariness. Were it not for the bars, it could almost be the same building. Billy and Nik walked nervously, without a word, Billy clutching the gold watch in his pocket until it clung to his sweaty palm.

The jailer led them to a cell occupied by a woman who looked roughly the same age as Aunt Catherine. In spite of her surroundings and meager attire, it was clear that she was trying very hard to keep up appearances. When her eyes met Uncle Will's, she sprang forward and clutched the bars of her cell.

"Mr. Sheppard!" Her voice carried an unmistakable American Southern drawl.

Uncle Will reached up and took her hand. "Florie, are you all right?"

"All things considered." She tried to force a smile.

By now the jailer had withdrawn to the end of the corridor; but he continued to keep a sharp eye on Florie Maybrick's visitors. Billy and Nik leaned quietly against the cold stone wall opposite the cell.

Uncle Will spoke in low tones. "What happened?"

Florie's eyes immediately filled with tears. She gasped and clapped her hand over her mouth in an attempt to regain some composure.

"I...I don't know, Mr. Sheppard. I just don't know. Jim was so sick. They're saying I poisoned him. But it's just not true! I know things weren't..." She trailed off into sobs. Uncle Will said nothing.

"Maybe it was my fault," she continued. "Our marriage was not...what it should have been. We kept up appearances. But..." At this point, Florie stared into space, seeming to become detached from what she was saying, as if it were the only way to get the words out.

"I was unfaithful." She bowed her head and continued sobbing. "He was always traveling to London and..."

"I don't understand," Uncle Will whispered. "Are you saying it was suicide?"

Florie looked up. "I can't be sure. He was so sick, and getting sicker all the time. I found a vial of arsenic in his desk one day. He kept saying strange things. Like he was trying to confess to something himself."

"Like what?"

"He said...he would not be blamed for nothing." She paused, trying to understand what she had just said. "He said that many times. He would not be blamed for nothing. What did he mean?" Her eyes searched Uncle Will's. "What did he do?"

Uncle Will shrugged. "What else did he say?" he asked.

"One night...he said..." Again, Florie covered her face with her hands. She drew a deep breath. "He said that he was beyond the grace of God!"

Uncle Will's eyes widened, and he turned to look at the two boys. They had been listening intently the entire time. Their expressions were stiff.

"Mr. Sheppard," Florie pleaded, "what did he do?! Have I driven him to do something horrible? Please tell me!"

Uncle Will tried to calm her as best as he could; but he really had nothing to offer.

"Florie, I don't know what he's done, or if he's even done anything. Those were probably just hasty words, spoken in a fit of rage. I promise you, Florie, I'll do what I can to find out what happened. I can't promise you any more than that."

"Is he really beyond the grace of God?" she asked.

Uncle Will hesitated. Billy saw a pained look cross his face. Uncle Will turned back toward Florie and smiled weakly. She clasped his hand. Uncle Will turned to leave, but she held on to his hand.

"Am I?"

Uncle Will looked directly into her eyes.

"Of course not!"

She closed her eyes and squeezed his hand before releasing it.

"Mr. Sheppard," her voice sounded determined, "if you can, would you tell my children that I love them, and that we'll be together again soon?"

"I'll do what I can."

Within fifteen minutes, Uncle Will and the boys emerged from the building. Uncle Will bore an unmistakable look of dismay.

"I'm guessing that raised more questions than it answered," Billy remarked.

Uncle Will nodded, and then walked down the steps to the waiting coach.

"She's being railroaded!" Uncle Will hissed, "And I'm convinced that Janus is behind it."

"What do we do now?" asked Nik.

"Can't we just go back a couple of years and find this Maybrick guy?" Billy added. "Maybe we can get the watch from him and even save his life!"

Uncle Willie held his hand up. "We can't do that. His death and his wife's trial are already recorded history. As I reminded you, we can't simply go back and change that. Who knows what future events we would irreparably alter by doing that?"

"I guess you have a point," Billy answered.

Uncle Will shouted out the window to the driver, "Do you know the way to Battlecrease House in Aigburth?"

"Of course," the portly coachman replied, "it's become quite the attraction!"

They headed south along the River Mersey toward Battlecrease House, the former home of the Maybricks. The large, grayish house stood across the road from the cricket grounds. It looked neglected and desolate, despite the fact that it had only been vacated a short time ago, and its contents recently sold at auction. Uncle Will and the boys stepped off the coach and approached the front door. To their surprise, it was unlocked. Once inside, Uncle Will called out to see if anyone was in the building. Since no answer came, they commenced to explore the empty rooms, their footsteps echoing off the bare walls and floors. Nik noticed a sheet of crumpled paper lying on the floor and picked it up. Unfolding it, he showed it to the others. It contained words written in a very unsteady hand, with ink splattered across most of the letters, reading:

"Tempus Omnia Relevat"

"What does that mean?" he asked.

"Time reveals all," Uncle Will answered. "It was inscribed on one of the watches."

Nik put the paper back where he found it, and they continued their exploration of the house. Their search of the first floor revealed nothing more than that scrap of paper; so they made their way to the second floor. All the rooms were empty. Soon, they had made their way to the attic, kicking up great plumes of dust from the rough wood plank floor. The sunlight streaming in through the small windows and illuminating the dust clouds reminded Billy of that afternoon in the workshop, when Uncle Will first gave him the watch. As their eyes adjusted to the relative darkness, they stepped carefully across the creaking floor. Suddenly, Nik stumbled into Billy, nearly knocking him over.

"Look where you're going, you klutz!" Billy exclaimed.

"Sorry," Nik said, regaining his balance. "The floor is uneven..."

As he said that, he looked down to see why. Where he planted his foot just a moment ago, one of the wood planks had dislodged, revealing a small space under the floor. All eyes were on the hole as Nik bent down to pull away the loose board. He reached down and lifted out a scrapbook. It had a black cover and quarter-bound leather spine. A look at the edge revealed that some of the pages had been removed. Nik opened the book carefully, expecting, as the others were, to see photographs. Instead they saw page after page of handwriting, some of which was crossed out. Some of the writing appeared to be poetry; the rest had the appearance of a journal. Nik's eyes scanned a page as he began to read aloud:

"Arise Sir Jack she will say, and now you can go as you may. Jim, Jack, Jack, Jim. Ha ha ha."

He lowered the book and looked quizzically at Uncle Will.

"Let's have a look, boy." Uncle Will took the book and thumbed through it. "It looks like Maybrick's writing." He continued to thumb through the book, his expression growing ever more pained as he went. He read aloud: "It has been far too long since my last. I have been unwell. I am in the habit of taking strong medicine. Will visit the city very soon, very soon." Uncle Will looked up at the boys, surprised as they were at the contents of this book. Finally, he turned to the last page. As he read it silently, he suddenly gasped, nearly dropping the book in horror.

"Uncle Will, what's up?!" Billy rushed closer to him.

"Listen to this," was the shaky reply. Uncle Will continued to read:

> *"I place this now in a place where it shall be found. I pray whoever should read this will find it in their heart to forgive me. Remind all, whoever you may be, that I was once a gentle man. May the Good Lord have mercy on my soul, and forgive me for all I have done. I give my name that all know of me, so history do tell, what love can do to a gentle man born.*
>
> *Yours truly.*
> *Jack the Ripper.*
> *Dated this third day of May 1889."*

There followed an eerie silence, as the boys stood frozen, digesting what they had just heard. Uncle Will lowered the book, closed his eyes, and let it fall to the floor. The sudden thump jarred the boys back to their senses.

"I don't..." Billy started to say. He was interrupted by Uncle Will's raised hand. The old man was looking toward the entrance to the attic. The silence was broken by the muffled sound of voices downstairs. All three froze where they were, listening intently.

"Has everything been accounted for?" one voice asked. Billy and his uncle recognized it as Dr. Janus'.

"Yes, sir," replied another voice. "Except for the watch. Apparently, it was sold before we could get to it."

"That fool's family! They're behaving like vultures."

"We should be going, sir."

The voices were followed by the sound of the front door closing. Uncle Will waited for what seemed to the boys like several minutes and stealthily walked to the small window overlooking the street. He saw a dark figure moving along the sidewalk. Looking across the street, he saw that the coach was still waiting for him and the boys. They breathed a collective sigh of relief and made their way out the front door.

They soon returned to the mansion, with Uncle Will still visibly agitated. He stormed into the library and tossed his jacket across the back of his chair. The boys stood in the arched doorway, unsure of whether or not to get comfortable. Uncle Will paced the floor in front of the fireplace. Soon Aunt Catherine and Gwyneth entered from the upper gallery, making their way down the spiral staircase.

"What's wrong, William?" Aunt Catherine asked.

Aside from making eye contact with her, he all but ignored her. He paced across the room and stood with folded arms in front of the globe, staring at it. Aunt Catherine and Gwyneth approached the boys, and they all exchanged concerned glances.

Aunt Catherine asked, "What happened?"

Billy began to respond, "We went to Maybrick's..."

"Boys," Uncle Will interrupted, "we need to track down that watch. He must have taken it to London." He never took his eyes off the globe. Billy stepped to his uncle's side and stared at the globe with him. He noticed Uncle Will was looking at London.

"So that's where we're headed," Billy assumed.

Uncle Will paused for a moment before he answered.

"I might as well show you how this thing works."

With that, he turned to the small metal box at the end of the gimbal and began to operate the crystal knobs. Billy could see that each knob was labeled to correspond to dates, months, and years. Once Uncle Will had it set to November 9, 1888, he began to turn the crank. With a loud metallic clatter, the globe began to rotate in its gimbal. The concentric rings around it began to rotate as well, crossing over each other at the same time. Soon, the cranking stopped, and the two brass pointers came to rest, one pointing at Leeds, the other at London.

"Perfect," Uncle Will said.

"Let's go, Nik," Billy called. He turned to see Nik sitting on the sofa, listening intently to whatever Gwyneth was telling him. Billy had to repeat himself to get Nik's attention. Nik appeared disappointed.

"Billy, Mister Sheppard, if it is all right with you, I would like to stay behind for now."

Uncle Will raised an eyebrow and looked at Billy. Before either of them could respond, Aunt Catherine spoke up.

"You are most welcome to stay here, Nikolai." She glanced at Uncle Will. "Don't worry, William. The three of us will be fine." Gwyneth was visibly pleased with her mother's decision.

Realizing there was no point in pressing the issue, Uncle Will turned to Billy. Billy was already opening the watch.

"Behave yourself, Nik;" Uncle Will said with a grin, "I may not be gone very long."

Chapter Eleven

Billy and Uncle Will found themselves in a dark, flat, grassy area, dark because it was night when they arrived in London. Billy's eyes adjusted slowly to the darkness. The faint glow of gas lamps was visible in the distance, each one haloed by the fog in the air.

"Where are we?" he asked.

"Hyde Park," was the answer. Uncle Will walked purposefully toward the lights. "Stick close," he reminded Billy.

Soon after their exit from the park into the poorly lit London streets, Billy found himself sitting across from Uncle Will in a pub. The place reeked of beer, stale food, smoke, and bodies that had obviously not seen a bathtub in quite a while. Before him sat a plate of food that made him long for what Ben Franklin had served him. He didn't touch it. Uncle Will had only eaten part of his meal. He was working on a pint of stout. Billy's pint, like his dinner, went untouched. He had tasted beer before, sneaking a swig of it at the occasional unchaperoned party he'd attended, but this was far worse than anything he'd tasted before.

Part of Billy's lack of appetite stemmed from Uncle Will's demeanor. He had scarcely made eye contact with Billy since they left Maybrick's house. Billy was growing impatient with the discomfort this place was inflicting upon him.

"What are we doing here? I thought we were looking for Maybrick."

Uncle Will put down his pint and wiped the froth from his lips. He spoke softly.

"We need to lay low until dawn. If the diary is true, Jack the Ripper will claim his last victim between now and then. If our timing is right..."

Billy interrupted, "We can intercept him and save her, right?"

"Wrong."

For the first time all night, Uncle Will looked Billy in the eye.

"As I've told you, we cannot interfere with recorded history. We have no idea what effect it will have."

A pained look crossed Billy's face as he tried to take in what Uncle Will was telling him. This was insane. If he understood Uncle Will, they were going to let an innocent woman die just so they could find a missing watch. He said as much.

Uncle Will drew a deep breath. "Billy, I didn't say this was going to be pretty. I'd love to tell you that we're going to skip through all of history, righting every wrong, fixing every mistake, deciding who gets to live and who gets to die; but that's not how this works. I'm sorry, but history records that a prostitute named Mary Jane Kelly died on the morning of November 9, 1888. That's exactly what is going to happen. That's just the way it is."

Billy slumped back in his chair as Uncle Will drained the last of his pint. Uncle Will placed a few coins on the table, and they both exited the pub. Soon they were aboard a carriage, taking them, as Uncle Will had requested, to Dorsett Street in the Whitechapel district. By the time they reached their destination, the sun was rising. It cast a pale, misty light through the dilapidated row houses.

From Dorsett Street, Uncle Will led Billy on foot toward a narrow alley between two brick buildings. At this point, Billy was glad he hadn't eaten. The air in the alley was heavy with the stench of stale urine, and he certainly would have lost his meal. They quickly emerged from the end of the alley into a tiny street. Uncle Will looked toward one end of the street and then to the other.

As Billy's eyes followed Uncle Will's, they came upon a figure in the distance, crouching low against the stone wall of a building. Uncle Will approached the figure and Billy followed. As they drew closer, Billy could see that it was a man in a long dark coat. He was visibly shaking. Billy hesitated as his uncle drew even closer to the man.

"James?" Uncle Will ventured. The man responded by quietly laughing. Almost immediately, the laughter turned to sobbing. He began to fitfully rub his hands together. Billy saw that the man's hands were completely red. Billy wished he'd stayed behind with Nik.

"James!" Uncle Will snapped. His shoulders began to heave as his breathing raced.

The man lifted his head, but did not look at Uncle Will. Billy could now see his dark, lifeless eyes and the black mustache that covered his upper lip.

"James is the man who will not be blamed for nothing," he strained out between sobs. He tried even harder to tear the blood from his hands. His sobbing turned again to laughter. "James, Jack, Jack, James..."

Suddenly, Uncle Will lunged forward and seized James by his coat. He lifted him to his feet and slammed him against the wall. A look of anguish covered James' face, and he began sobbing again.

"James, what have you done?!" Uncle Will demanded.

James was now weeping freely. "I couldn't stop it! I couldn't make it stop! I loved her so much, but I couldn't make it stop!!"

"The watch, James," Uncle Will barked, shaking James violently, "what have you done with it." James did not answer, so Uncle Will repeated his interrogation. When that failed to produce the desired result, Uncle Will released him, and he fell to the ground.

"You fool!" Uncle Will spat. "You could have come to me for help. You could have come to any one of us."

James knelt sobbing against the wall. Uncle Will began to pace, straightening his glasses. Billy leaned with one arm against a wall on the opposite side of the street, wanting desperately to leave.

"I am damned," James said with unsettling clarity. "I am truly damned. I am beyond the grace of God." He began sobbing again. "The watch is gone."

Uncle Will stopped pacing and stared open-mouthed at the broken Maybrick. He stepped slowly toward the man. Maybrick cowered. He blurted out his explanation.

"William, forgive me! I had to do it. The temptation was too great!" James gazed at his hands, no less stained with blood than before. "I couldn't allow this blasphemy to spread beyond this place – this time! Oh, God, have mercy!"

"What have you done with the watch?!"

"I sold it," James whispered.

"You sold it?!" Uncle Will was incredulous.

"I sold it to a man named Redgrave. Michael Redgrave. He knows nothing of the watch's power."

Uncle Will grabbed James by the coat again and lifted him. He placed his face directly in front of Maybrick's.

"You idiot! You've ruined us! Janus will find it, and then no one will be able to keep up with him."

"Forgive me, William," James sobbed.

"Go!"

Uncle Will released him, and he dropped into the gutter, landing in a puddle of unimaginable filth.

"Go and meet your destiny, James Maybrick. May God forgive you!"

As Billy observed, James pulled himself to his feet and stumbled down the street, dragging the tails of his coat through the mud as he went. At one point, he fell headlong onto the pavement, collected himself, and continued his retreat. Uncle Will and Billy stood silently watching Maybrick until he was out of sight.

Billy turned back toward the alley. Uncle Will was soon at his side. They walked slowly.

"Now what are we going to do?" Billy asked.

"I don't know yet."

At that moment, they were interrupted by a noise coming from the street where they had been a few moments ago. It was the clattering of empty bottles. Billy stepped to the end of the alley and carefully peered around the corner. Before he could notice anything, he was nearly knocked to the ground by a boy stumbling into the alley. Both were equally startled by each other's presence. The boy's eyes locked with Billy's for a fleeting moment. They were wide with shock. The boy's face was pale. The front of his jacket was stained with vomit. Billy winced at the boy's acrid breath. Before he could react any further, the boy took off down the alley.

"Murder! Murder!" the boy screamed.

Billy stepped onto the narrow street from where the boy had come. He looked along the wall to his right and noticed the corner of a tattered curtain hanging through the frame of a window. The window was missing a pane near the bottom. A crumpled coat, which had not been there before, lay under the window. Billy could hear the buzzing of houseflies emanating from the open window. He startled when Uncle Will placed a hand on his shoulder.

"Come on, Billy. There's nothing you can do for her now."

Billy's breathing became labored as he began to imagine the carnage behind that window. He ached to understand what Uncle Will had told him at the pub. Uncle Will, without another word, led him back toward Dorsett Street. Soon, they were making their way out of Whitechapel.

Just as they reached the river, a voice was heard behind them.

"Constable! That's the man who took my watch!"

The two turned to see a short, dark haired, slender man in a dark suit, standing some distance away. A police officer was several paces behind him. Billy looked at the man and recoiled. It was the same man he had seen riding down the road when they were walking to Philadelphia. More shocking than that, it was the same man he had seen talking to his mother in the days before Uncle Will was put in the hospital. As their eyes met, the man gave Billy a satisfied grin.

"Peters!" Uncle Will hissed.

Peters stepped aside to make way for the policeman, who was running down the sidewalk toward them. All at once, they turned and fled. The air was pierced by the shriek of the policeman's whistle as he summoned assistance. Uncle Will and Billy rounded the corner and continued along another street. They could hear the pounding of several feet coming up the sidewalk behind them. They rounded another corner and proceeded along a narrow alley between two houses, briefly losing sight of their pursuers.

"Billy," Uncle Will wheezed, "get us out of here!" He pointed toward the sunlight that shone in a narrow shaft along the alley. Billy took the watch from his pocket and opened it, grabbing the stem with shaking hands.

"Where..."

"Just get us out of here!"

Chapter Twelve

Uncle Will and Billy found themselves tumbling through the darkness, being struck from all sides by what they soon realized were cornstalks. The hole closed behind them, leaving their pursuers to wonder what had happened to them. When all was still, Uncle Will stood up and brushed the dirt and husks from his clothing. Billy tried to pick himself up, but he was thoroughly entangled in a stalk he had uprooted. Uncle Will quickly assisted him. Their eyes adjusted to the bright moonlight that illuminated the field.

"Where are we?" Billy asked.

"You're asking me?" Uncle Will responded. "Give me that watch."

Billy handed the watch to his uncle, who opened it to check the date.

"1965. Well, that tells us when. The question remains 'where.'"

Uncle Will began to pick his way carefully through the standing corn, followed close behind by his nephew. He cautioned Billy not to allow himself to be seen by anyone, since they were still dressed for 1889. They continued to move quietly through the field. In the distance, the moonlight reflected off a church steeple. Billy pointed this out to Uncle Will, who stopped short and studied it carefully.

"I know where we are," he announced in a whisper. "We couldn't have done it again, even if we tried."

"So where are we?" Billy asked insistently.

"We're back in Cannon Falls," Uncle Will answered, pointing in another direction. "Our house is over in that direction. It looks a lot nicer around here without all those cookie cutter houses they built, or should I say 'they're going to build.'"

Billy grinned proudly at his accomplishment as they continued to make their way out of the field. Soon they came to a narrow dirt road that cut through the field, its potholes filled with the remains of the last rainfall. As they moved quietly along the road, Uncle Will again stopped short. His eyes widening, he put out his hand to stop Billy as well. He directed Billy back into the rows of corn. Just as Billy was about to ask why, Uncle Will pointed down the road. In the distance, Billy could make out the shape of a car, parked in the road. The glow from the dashboard lights was visible through the mist-covered windows, as were the silhouettes of two people inside the car. Billy began to quietly chuckle.

"They're making out, aren't they?"

Uncle Will nodded in response. He seemed to Billy to be turning pale, but his expression did not change.

"We have to get away from here - very quietly," Uncle Will admonished.

"I don't understand..." Billy whispered.

Uncle Will grabbed his nephew by the arm and clamped his other hand over Billy's mouth, dragging him back toward the rows of corn. Once they had moved away from the spot, Uncle Will released him. Billy noticed that Uncle Will was sweating profusely.

"What's going on?" Billy hissed.

"I just realized it. Those are your grandparents, Billy," Uncle Will explained. "Let's just say it would really ruin my day if they were disturbed right now."

With that, he rose and disappeared into the corn. Billy stared blankly at the space his uncle had just vacated, unsure of whether to feel shock or embarrassment.

The two walked some distance through the cornfield. It seemed longer than it actually was, because the rows of corn made for slow progress. Eventually, they came to a small knoll in the middle of the field. At the center of it stood a dead tree, half of which was lying, partially buried, in the dirt. The ground was relatively smooth here, so Uncle Will and Billy sat down.

"We'll have to wait here until daybreak," said Uncle Will. "Then we need to get back to Gwyneth, Catherine, and Nik. If Janus could get that close to us, he just might be able to find them."

"But Uncle Will," Billy responded, "we left the computer back at the mansion. How are we going to calculate for the trip back?"

"We'll just have to wing it. Since we're returning to where we just came from, we should end up pretty close to it. The few hours between now and sunrise shouldn't make too much difference. We'd better get some rest."

Uncle Will leaned back against the tree and closed his eyes. Billy looked with resignation at him, and soon he was asleep.

A short while later, Billy found that the hard earth was no substitute for his own bed. He woke up and unconsciously began to rub the back of his neck. As he turned over, he saw that Uncle Will was wide awake, still looking agitated. In fact, he was standing against the dead tree, gazing upward toward the stars. He stood and approached his uncle.

"Can't sleep?"

"Hmm?" Uncle Will turned with a slight start. "Oh, I was just thinking."

"About what?"

"Nothing really."

"You haven't said much since we found that diary," Billy noted. "You also haven't said much more about Marcus."

Uncle Will sighed. "It's not easy to see decent, brilliant men go mad."

"No, it's not."

Uncle Will could see that Billy meant him as well.

"I suppose none of this has been easy for you either, and I'm sorry for that."

Billy looked at the ground and nodded.

"You're concerned that I'm going to end up like them."

Again, Billy nodded, listening to the rhythmic chirping of crickets. Uncle Will had said exactly what Billy was feeling. Billy thought about their experience at Briarcliff, and it was not hard to imagine Uncle Will becoming the sad specimen of human debris to which Marcus had been reduced. What scared him even more was the fact that a member of this 'Guild' Uncle Will spoke so fondly of spent his last days as history's most notorious serial killer. His expression betrayed his feelings.

"Billy," Uncle Will assured, "I have not gone crazy."

"I'm starting to understand that," replied Billy. "There's one thing that made me realize that."

"What's that?"

"The man you called Peters. He's the guy that Mom and Dad were talking to about you."

"Yes, I know." This response surprised Billy.

"You mean you knew all along you were being sent there?"

"Well, I figured that's how Janus would try to neutralize me. It seems to have worked where Marcus, Rupert and James were concerned."

"Why didn't Janus just kill you and the others?"

"I'm not sure," answered Uncle Will. "Maybe he had other plans for us. Maybe he was satisfied with simply making us appear insane. That way, even if we managed to tell anyone before he killed us; we'd be dismissed as crazy. It's a pretty common ploy. If you can't just eliminate someone, then make the person seem like a lunatic." Uncle Will cracked a smile and shifted his stance.

"I once knew a test pilot who was stationed at an airbase where the first jet fighters were being tested. The airbase itself wasn't a secret, but the project was. To keep the other pilots from talking about it, he'd go up in the jet sometimes wearing a gorilla mask and a derby hat, smoking a cigar!"

"What was that all about?" asked Billy.

"Just try to imagine a pilot claiming he'd seen some fantastic new aircraft while on patrol or training. Mind you, up to then, all our planes had propellers and couldn't move as fast as a jet. This thing comes up alongside him, and there's my friend with the mask and the hat and the cigar, waving at him. The poor guy doesn't dare mention it to anyone! Can't you just hear him trying to describe the thing?! When asked who was at the controls, the guy would have to admit he was seeing things." Uncle Will let out a hearty chuckle. Billy laughed too, but more out of relief than anything. He realized that his uncle was probably the sanest man he knew.

He thought for a moment. "Do you think Janus smashed that watch, or was it Marcus?"

"My guess is that it was Marcus," Uncle Will answered. "Janus wouldn't have gone to that much trouble just to destroy the watch. No, I think Marcus knew that Janus was on to him, so he destroyed it to keep Janus from getting it. It was probably the smartest thing he's ever done."

"What about James Maybrick?" Billy asked.

"After talking with his wife, I can only assume what happened. Apparently, he was addicted to arsenic."

"Arsenic? Isn't that poison?"

"Yes, in certain quantities. Back then, it was often used, in small doses, as a narcotic, or for certain medical purposes. Anyway, I have little doubt as to how Janus used this addiction to his own advantage. Then he simply had her framed for murder to try and gain access to the watch, as we heard while we were hiding in the attic at Battlecrease House."

"What about what James Maybrick said about being beyond the grace of God?"

Uncle Will looked down. "What about it?"

"Is he?"

"Billy," Uncle Will said, "you know better than to ask such a ridiculous question."

Billy was persistent. "Well?"

Uncle Will sighed. "I don't know the man's heart. All I can say is that he would not be beyond God's grace unless he chose to be. I just don't know."

"Uncle Will?" Billy began.

After a long pause Uncle Will locked his eyes with Billy's.

Billy looked down. "Nothing."

At that moment, Uncle Will's attention was turned to a glimmer of light in the distance. A pair of taillights was visible through the rows of corn. They moved toward the far end of the field to a dirt road and off into the night. Billy glanced at his uncle and saw him let out a deep breath. A look of profound relief crossed Uncle Will's face as he tracked his parents' departure.

"You know, Uncle Will," Billy said, "there's one thing you haven't told me. How did you ever get involved with this Guild in the first place?"

"Gosh, that was years ago." Uncle Will shifted his eyes and let out a faint laugh.

"I was the owner of a small antique shop at the time. 'Junk shop' would be a more accurate description. Anyway, I got a package one day. It contained a watch and an old sheet of paper with instructions. It described the purpose of the Guild, explaining that we were all from different time periods and backgrounds, that we were only to observe, but never alter, human events. The watches were deliberately separated from each other, by time as well as location. The Guild rarely met as a group. We usually met in pairs, and we never used any two watches at the same place and time. The intention was to keep us from interfering with each other. I've already told you how Janus and Peters wanted to do more than just observe."

Uncle Will paused and let out a deep breath, then continued.

"They say that power corrupts, and absolute power corrupts absolutely. Janus is looking for absolute power in controlling time itself."

"I just can't believe that Mom and Dad are going along with this guy," Billy whispered.

"Now just a minute, boy," Uncle Will said sternly. "Your parents are completely ignorant of Janus and his motives. They thought they were acting in my best interests. I couldn't tell them the truth about him, or Peters; so I had to go along with it."

"So you gave me the watch."

"Exactly."

"So that leaves just one more watch, assuming that Janus has just one."

"We can't assume anything at this point. Janus has got to be stopped."

Billy noticed the seriousness in Uncle Will's face, and realized what he meant.

"You mean..."

Uncle Will gazed at Billy knowingly over the top of his eyeglasses.

Chapter Thirteen

The following morning found Uncle Will and Billy back at the mansion in Leeds. Aunt Catherine was surprised to see them returning so soon and assumed that their trip to London was aborted, since they had only been gone a few minutes. Uncle Will was quick to correct her and explained as best he could what had happened. Even Billy was having a hard time keeping all the traveling they had done sorted in his head. Gwyneth was ecstatic to see them both back safely. She embraced her father just as she had before. Nik was visibly disappointed.

The reunited family spent the rest of the day lazing about the house, doing as little as possible. Gwyneth sat at the grand piano that stood at the far end of the library, playing and singing from a hymnbook. The rest simply sat and relaxed. Billy nodded off to sleep at the end of the sofa. The exception was Uncle Will, who spent the time poring over books in his library.

Later that afternoon, a groggy Billy sat at a large oak desk in what had become his room at the mansion. It was somewhat the same size as his own room at home, but more elaborately furnished. The bed was large enough, he thought, for three or four people. A tall oak wardrobe stood in one corner, and a matching washstand in the other. The desk stood before a bay window hung with lace curtains. On the desk, in front of him, was Uncle Will's portable computer. Billy opened it and turned it on. After a few tiny beeps and the whir of the hard disk, its screen flashed the words:

ENTER PASSWORD:

Billy hesitated for a moment, trying to guess what that password might be. He typed on the tiny keypad the words:

TEMPUS FUGIT

The computer answered back:

ACCESS DENIED

Billy tried a number of other words, including the names of the other watches, names of Guild members he knew of, even his own name. The response from the computer was still the same:

ACCESS DENIED

Defeated, Billy leaned back in his chair and gazed absently out the window. The window offered a wide view of the property behind the mansion. He could see the entire flower garden with its reflecting pool, sparkling in the sunset. On one end of the garden, he saw Gwyneth picking some flowers to display on the dinner table that evening. He could also see Uncle Will and Aunt Catherine strolling across the lawn outside the garden, arm in arm, the two dogs at their heels. He looked again at Gwyneth, then at the computer in front of him. Grinning, he typed her name. The computer responded.

ORBITAL DISPLACEMENT CALCULATION SYSTEM.
PLEASE ENTER STARTING POINT COORDINATES.

The computer presented Billy with a map of the world, divided by a grid of very small squares. Major cities were clearly labeled. He pressed a few keys to move a tiny arrow to his approximate location on the map. After he pressed the 'ENTER' key, the computer asked for the year he was in, then the year to which he wanted to go. For fun, he typed in the year he was born, and was promptly disappointed to see that the computer placed him in the center of the Atlantic Ocean. At that moment, he heard Nik's voice behind him.

"What are you up to?" he asked. He had been in the library, looking through the books.

"I'm just fooling around with this thing."

"Let me have a try at it?"

As the two boys experimented with the computer, they found that if they simply entered the starting point and the destination, the computer would calculate what date they would arrive. They began to enter all sorts of exotic destinations to see when they might get to them. Finally, Nik typed in his hometown of Asbest. The computer came back with the date:

JULY, 1918

"Wow," Billy said. "That's not too far from the time we were at Buckingham Palace."

When he didn't hear a response right away, he turned to see Nik staring, wide-eyed, at the screen.

"What?"

Nik pointed at the screen. Close to the city of Asbest was the city of Ekaterinburg.

Billy asked, "What's that? Eka... Ek..."

"Ekaterinburg," Nik replied. "July, 1918. That is where Tsar Nicholas and his family were murdered by the Bolsheviks!"

Billy sat thinking about what Nik said, trying to grasp the significance the event had for the two of them. Suddenly, it occurred to him. They both spoke at once.

"Anastasia!"

Both minds where whirling with the realization of what happened, or in their case, what would happen. Billy shook his head.

"Wait a minute. Are you thinking what I'm thinking?"

"That depends on what you're thinking," replied Nik.

Billy thrust his hand into his pocket, pulled out the watch, and sat studying it for a moment.

Chapter Fourteen

When Billy opened his eyes, he thought for a moment that he was looking at a black-and-white photograph. Everything around him seemed to be gray, of one shade or another. The air was dry and filled with dust. He had to blink a couple of times to clear it out of his eyes. He glimpsed Nik taking a few steps ahead of him. From the moment they stepped through the hole, Billy heard an incessant wailing sound. When he turned to one side, he finally realized that he was hearing someone scream.

The boys found themselves standing in the middle of a plowed field. The furrows stretched away from them, punctuated with short bare stalks of what was supposed to be wheat. About fifty feet away from them, an old woman was sprawled across a furrow, staring wide-eyed at them, holding herself up with one arm and frantically crossing herself with the other. She was dressed in what amounted to rags. Her skirts were covered in a thick layer of the same dust that blew through the air. Next to her laid a sack of small stalks, half of them spilled on the dusty ground. Billy and Nik looked at each other, studying each other's faces for some suggestion of what to do next. They clearly hadn't planned on this. Nik started toward her, holding out his hand in a futile gesture of reassurance. The woman scrambled to her feet. She staggered backward then wheeled around and tried to run as fast as her aged body would allow. She was shouting something in Russian. Billy didn't understand it, anymore than he could understand what Nik was trying to say to her, but he could tell that it was the same word, repeated over and over.

"What's she saying?" He caught up to Nik and grabbed him by the shoulder.

Nik sighed. "Demons. She keeps saying 'demons.' That is what she thinks we are."

The old woman kept running until she was no longer in sight. The boys stood still, trying to figure out what to do next.

"We'd better get out of here," Billy said.

"That would seem obvious," was the reply.

They decided that moving in the opposite direction of the old woman's horrified departure would be the best course of action. They didn't want any more such unwanted attention. Walking for what seemed like an hour, they approached a small village.

"Any idea where we are?" Billy asked.

"None whatsoever," Nik answered.

They continued until they reached the center of the village. The street was populated by a few small shops, and by even fewer people. Nik noticed a man leaning against the doorpost of one of the shops. The man had a long thin face as furrowed as the field they had just come from. Smoke curled from a small, hand-rolled cigarette between his lips. The man scratched his head under his wool cap, eyeing the boys suspiciously. Nik put his hand on Billy's shoulder, stopped him, and approached the man. Billy heard them exchange a few words in Russian, and soon Nik was returning.

"He said there is a truck taking some men to a workers' rally," he explained. "It leaves in half an hour."

As the truck bounced along, Billy and Nik were having a difficult time finding a comfortable way to sit on the hard splintered planks that made up the floor. This was not helped by the fact that their clothing was drawing stares from the other passengers. It was not so much the style, which was still passable despite being about thirty years out of date; but rather it was the fact that their clothes were in such good condition. Nearly all the others in the back of the truck were dressed in worn-out work clothes. Finally, a tall, young man sitting next to Nik leaned over and broke the tension with a question. Nik listened carefully, and then responded in what seemed to Billy like a very careful tone. It was clear that Nik was trying to avoid raising anyone's suspicion.

"What's up?" he asked when the conversation was over.

"He wanted to know where we are from. I told him we were students from abroad, trying to find one of my relatives."

"Students from abroad? That's original."

"He wanted to know why you didn't speak Russian."

"So what did you tell him?"

Nik smiled. "I told him you were the bourgeois son of a wealthy industrial baron. Now, relax!"

Billy's expression turned sour. "That's not funny, Nik."

The ride continued without another word between them, until the scenery outside told them that they were approaching a large city. The lengthening shadows told them that it was getting late. They both hoisted themselves up to look around, each wincing at the stiffness in their joints. Billy spotted a sign by the edge of the road. Although the single word on the sign was in Cyrillic, he had a fair idea of what it said. He asked Nik for confirmation.

"Does that say what I hope it says?"

"Ekaterinburg," was the reply.

"We'd better get out here," said Billy quietly, "since we don't need a whole truckload of revolutionaries knowing what we're up to."

The boys looked at each other and nodded. Nik made his way to the front of the truck and thumped the roof of the cab with his open hand. He called to the driver in Russian, and soon the truck lumbered to a stop. Billy and Nik hopped out the back, waved to the other passengers and made for a wooded area near the edge of town. Soon enough, darkness began to appear behind the mountains to the east as the sun set behind them. Billy stopped and knelt down, taking the orbital displacement calculator from inside his jacket. He started tapping on the keys, looking around cautiously to see that no one observed him. Nik immediately understood this, and kept watch as well.

"I'm trying to figure out how we're going to get back once we find her," Billy said. "I think I'm finally getting the hang of this thing. If I'm reading it right, we shouldn't be too far from my uncle's house when we go back. We just have to make sure we leave from this spot."

Nik nodded, and then looked around. Taking a white handkerchief from his pocket, he tied it to a nearby branch.

"That should help us find it later."

Billy closed the cover on the orbital displacement calculator and placed it back inside his jacket. Then, the boys headed into the woods, keeping the edge of the city in view just beyond the trees. It wasn't long before night fell, and they found it very slow going, trying to pick their way through. Billy wished he had thought to bring a flashlight. At present, he would have been happy with a book of matches.

"We're never going to find it! We should have just waited until morning," he complained.

"Then she will already be dead," Nik was quick to point out.

Hours passed as they continued to slog their way through the forest, trying desperately to keep the lights of Ekaterinburg in view. The air was cold and damp, and the boys found themselves clutching their jackets around themselves. Eventually, they emerged from the woods at the edge of a narrow road that curved into the distance. They stopped to collect their bearings. As they did so, their attention was immediately drawn to the sound of a vehicle approaching from the direction of the city. Nik grabbed Billy by the shoulder and guided him back into the woods as the beams of two dull headlights shone on the spot where Billy was just standing. They boys crouched behind a thick tree and waited as a small truck rolled by.

It was similar to the truck that they had ridden in earlier, except that the back was completely enclosed. Billy hazarded a look from behind the tree and observed that the truck was seemingly full of people, mostly men from what he could see through its open back. At that moment, he caught a glimpse of something unusual in the center of the floor. Protruding from underneath a sheet of canvas was the unmistakable outline of a woman's hand. Its pale color stood in sharp contrast to its dark surroundings.

In an instant, the boys were on their feet. Billy fumbled to get the watch out of his pocket. He snapped it open with shaking hands, squinting as he held it close to his face.

"We are too late!" Nik exclaimed.

"It's nearly two in the morning," Billy confirmed. "Come on!"

Without another word, the two boys ran at full speed after the truck, which by now was out of sight. It didn't help that the road was rough and poorly maintained, or that their shoes were not made for running. The cool night air stung their throats as they gulped it down. It was not long before the two were completely out of breath and forced to slow down to a walk. Neither spoke as they continued to walk. The only sound was that of their tired feet shuffling across the gravel.

Suddenly, that sound was accompanied by the sounds of distant voices, shouting in Russian. Billy and Nik once again broke into a run to find the source of the noise. They soon spotted the glow of a bonfire and cautiously approached. They saw the silhouettes of men, some with rifles slung across their backs, carrying bodies from the truck. The men were placing the bodies near what appeared to be the entrance of a mineshaft. The boys tried to see who was still in the truck. They carefully picked their way through the trees and undergrowth, trying to get a better look. As they did, the men continued to unload the truck.

As much as Billy and Nik expected it, they were still horribly shaken by what they saw next. A man with a rifle reached into the truck and pulled out the limp body of Anastasia. Her face was contorted and covered in blood, as was her clothing. As the man pulled at her legs to slide her off the back of the truck, she suddenly convulsed and screamed. The sudden movement from what was supposed to be a corpse caught the soldier completely by surprise. He lost his footing in the mud and fell back, dropping her on the ground. Billy leapt to his feet and almost broke cover to get to her, but Nik was quick to restrain him. Billy had a hard time not simply throwing his friend to the ground. He wheeled around to confront Nik. Nik simply pointed back in the direction of the truck.

Anastasia was scrambling to her feet, and so was the soldier. She staggered toward the front of the truck, nearly sprawling face down in the mud as she did so. The long shadow of the truck cast by the bonfire helped to conceal her escape to everyone but Billy and Nik. Nik grabbed Billy by the arm and directed him in the same direction Anastasia was running. This brought them back into the thick woods. They ran along the tree line, keeping their heads low to avoid being spotted, and heading on a course that would intercept her escape. If not for the fact that she was tripping over the dead branches that littered the ground, she would have made it past them.

Nik was the first to reach her. He ran up along side her and threw his arms around her waist, knocking her to the ground. She cried out in pain, and Nik quickly clamped his hand over her mouth. Billy slid on his stomach to the spot where they had landed. Both of them look squarely into her terrified eyes. Nik whispered something to her in Russian, and before she could respond, he and Billy had lifted her to her feet. She promptly fell forward and groaned in pain. Nik rolled her over and scooped her up in his arms. Billy quickly gestured for Nik to go ahead of him; and despite the fact that carrying her made for slow going, Nik was quickly disappearing into the trees.

They could hear the shouts of the Russian soldiers who were pursuing them into the forest. For a moment, Nik slumped down behind a large tree, not once loosening his grip on Anastasia. Billy's eyes began to scan the ground, and soon his hands had to do the job. He found a rock, roughly the size of a softball, and lobbed it through the air. It arced through the woods until it struck the trunk of another tree a good distance away. It connected with a loud thump. The noise was followed by more shouts from the soldiers.

"I think it worked," Nik whispered. They soon realized the voices were headed away from them.

Nik struggled back to his feet, still cradling Anastasia. By now, she had lapsed into unconsciousness. They slowly picked their way through the forest. Billy stayed behind by several paces, constantly looking back and listening to make sure the Russians weren't following them. At once, he noticed that Nik and Anastasia were no longer in front of him. He stopped dead in his tracks and began to scan the woods all around him. His breath became heavy as it occurred to him that he had no idea where he was. He held his breath and tried to focus his hearing on any sound, but there was none.

His panic was relieved when he heard a faint whisper.

"Billy."

He turned slowly to find where it came from.

"Billy. Down here."

He turned again and saw Nik, from the shoulders up. Nik was standing in a ditch that ran through the woods. Billy was soon next to him. The ditch was probably a stream at one time or another. All that remained in the ditch were some rocks and a thick layer of soupy mud. The walls on either side were dry and crumbling. The top of the ditch was overgrown with tall grass and fallen branches. Nik had put Anastasia down against the bank he was hiding behind. The grass and partially eroded earth created a narrow canopy that covered them. Billy huddled down in the mud next to Anastasia, and Nik sat down on her other side.

She began to drift between complete unconsciousness and a rambling stupor, sometimes thrashing her arms and crying out. Nik spoke to her, trying to reassure her. Billy removed his jacket and placed it over her.

"It'll be dawn in a couple of hours," Billy said. "I hope we can still find our marker."

"I just hope she survives until then," Nik said.

Chapter Fifteen

A short while later, Uncle Will, Aunt Catherine, and Gwyneth returned to the house. Uncle Will made his way along the upstairs corridor to look for the boys. On the way, Billy intercepted him. He was perspiring and breathing heavily. His suit was very dirty. Uncle Will hardly had an opportunity to react when Billy spoke up.

"Uh...Uncle Will, don't freak out or anything, but..."

"But what?"

"Well...come with me. We've got a slight problem."

With that, Billy led his bewildered uncle down the corridor to his room. When he opened the door, Uncle Will rushed through, but was stopped dead by what he saw. Lying on the bed was the battered body of Anastasia, her dress splattered with blood and dirt. Her face was swollen, her lip bleeding profusely, her eyes blackened. She was shaking uncontrollably. Nik bent over her, trying in vain to brush aside her matted hair to examine her injuries. He spoke to her in Russian, but it was clear that she was not listening to him.

"Billy," a gaping Uncle Will said, "that's not..."

"It's...Anastasia," Billy replied hesitantly. "We found her just in time."

Uncle Will shook his head in exasperation, clapping his hand to his brow. "I don't believe this!"

Anastasia began to thrash about wildly, screaming in Russian. Nik had to nearly place his full weight on top of her to keep her on the bed. Billy ran to the washstand and filled the large porcelain bowl with water from the jug. Grabbing a towel, he brought both to the bedside. Nik dipped the towel in the water and attempted to clean the dirt and clotted blood from her face. Uncle Will regained his composure and called down the stairs to Aunt Catherine. She arrived seconds later, followed by Gwyneth. Both gasped at the sight of what was unfolding in their guestroom. Uncle Will barked out instructions to both of them, and they were out the door as quickly as they arrived.

A furious display of activity later, Anastasia was in somewhat better shape. Her bleeding had stopped, as did her wild convulsions, and her face was clear of grime, revealing the full extent of her injuries.

Uncle Will and the two boys, who were themselves bloodstained and grimy, moved into the hallway and closed the door. The two boys immediately sank to the floor. Uncle Will stood directly across from them, folding his arms, looking none too pleased.

"Boy," he addressed Billy sharply; "you have A LOT of explaining to do."

"It's a long story," replied a defeated Billy, his eyes squarely on the floor.

Uncle Will bent down, placing his face directly in front of his nephew's.

"I've got all the time in the world."

The boys commenced to relate the account of their recent adventure. They described how they had made the calculations and how they arrived in Asbest. They described how, thanks to Nik's fluent Russian and his albeit marginal knowledge of the area, they were able to make it all the way to the city of Ekaterinburg. They told how they followed the Bolsheviks into the forest where the bodies were to be buried, how Anastasia had not yet been killed, and how she escaped from the truck and ran. They then explained how they intercepted her in the forest, hid from the Bolsheviks until sunrise, and made it back to the bedroom.

Uncle Will listened patiently, and then he simply adjusted his glasses and turned to go downstairs. At that moment, Aunt Catherine and Gwyneth returned, carrying clean clothes and bandages for Anastasia. They entered the bedroom and closed the door behind them. Billy and Nik sat in silence on the hallway floor, unsure of what to do next. Soon, Billy rose and walked downstairs. Nik got up to follow, but Billy stopped and shook his head. Nik sat back down, knowing that what Billy was going to do he needed to do alone.

"I don't care what you thought!" Uncle Will was as angry as Billy had ever remembered seeing him. The veins in his neck stood out as he shook a condemning finger at Billy's face. "I told you that we couldn't do it, and I told you why; but you had to go and do it anyway! That's just great!"

"But...they were going to kill her!" Billy protested.

"They could have killed *you*, Billy! How would you suggest I explain that to your parents?"

Billy drew in a sudden breath. Only at that moment had he considered that possibility. The realization brought a lump to his throat, compelling him to swallow hard to keep from crying. The fact that his uncle, whom he loved and respected so much, was now furious with him didn't help. He bowed his head and began to sob.

"I'm sorry," was all he could choke out. He took the watch from his pocket and placed it on the heavy oak desk, turning his back to it.

Uncle Will stopped his tirade and stood across from Billy, lowering his head as well. He picked up the watch, took a deep breath, then stepped to Billy's side and put his arm around the boy.

"It's all right. I know you are."

Billy immediately tried to regain his composure, as any teenaged boy in his shoes would. He wiped his eyes on his sleeve.

"We were just trying to help her."

"I know, boy. I know how you feel. It's frustrating to know what's going to happen and sit back and do nothing; but you have to understand that it already did happen. You have to let it be."

"This whole thing is so crazy."

"I know."

Uncle Will sat in the chair by the fireplace, staring at the smoldering remains of the fire.

"Well, Billy," he said, "what's done is done. Have we figured out what we're going to do next?"

"I guess not," Billy replied, hanging his head in defeat.

Chapter Sixteen

The next morning, Billy sat on a rough stone bench at the edge of the garden, tossing the remains of a muffin to the ducks in the pool, watching them greedily snatch up the morsels. Gwyneth sat next to him, quietly swinging her feet back and forth under the bench. They were both startled when Aunt Catherine appeared suddenly at the entrance of the garden.

"Billy, Gwyneth! Come inside. Anastasia is awake!"

The two jumped off the bench and rushed into the house. Climbing the stairs to her room, they found her sitting up in bed. Next to the bed, a very tired Nik sat holding his head up with one hand. He had kept a vigil there the entire night, and so found it difficult not to nod off occasionally. He lifted his head with a start when Billy and Gwyneth entered. Aunt Catherine followed them into the room.

"She still needs to get some rest. She's gotten quite a beating."

Aunt Catherine hardly needed to mention such an obvious fact. Anastasia's face was still swollen on the left side, and both eyes were still slightly blackened. Where her lower lip was split and bleeding the night before, there was a telltale vertical scar. The white nightgown Aunt Catherine had provided for her concealed her other injuries. Aunt Catherine shook her head. After hearing from Uncle Will what had happened to her, she was amazed the girl was still alive.

"Where am I?" asked Anastasia, her voice shaking.

"You're in England," Nik replied. "You've been here all night."

At that moment, Uncle Will walked into the room. Seeing that she was awake, he approached the bed. Sitting on the edge of the bed, he removed his glasses.

"Do you remember what happened last night?" he asked her softly.

She paused a moment, glancing around the room. Suddenly, she began to breathe heavily, panting out soft phrases in Russian.

"What's she saying?" Billy whispered to Nik.

"It's coming back to her. She saw her father get shot. Then more shooting. She fell down. Felt something hit her. They were screaming."

In mid-sentence, she covered her face with her hands and sobbed loudly.

"Boys, Gwyneth, we'd better leave her alone for a while," Uncle Will said, ushering them out. "Catherine." He glanced at his wife, motioning toward Anastasia. Aunt Catherine sat on the edge of the bed and put her arms around the stricken girl, rocking her gently, as everyone else left the room.

The weeks that followed were spent mostly waiting for Anastasia to come to terms with what had happened to her family. The shock was further compounded by the realization that it was now the year 1889, that the two boys she had met in England had traveled through time to rescue her. The shock of such information, all at once, caused her recovery to take longer, and occasionally take a turn for the worse. Soon enough, though, she was able to leave the house and walk, with Billy's assistance, in the garden. Gwyneth was very adamant that Anastasia be allowed outside for fresh air. She also made sure that Anastasia's room at the house was constantly supplied with fresh flowers from the garden. When the boys and Uncle Will were busy around the estate, it was Gwyneth who made sure that Anastasia was comfortable and gainfully occupied.

Toward noon one day, Anastasia and Nik walked across the large grassy field beyond the garden. She was wearing a dress that belonged to Gwyneth, since her own clothing was too blood-stained and torn to salvage; aside from the fact that Aunt Catherine felt that her own clothes would remind her too much of what had happened to her and her family. In fact, the only readily apparent evidence of what she had been through was a one-inch scar that followed the contour of her left cheekbone. Several paces behind them, Billy and Gwyneth followed.

"She's doing so much better, Billy," Gwyneth said. "Father told me what happened. Imagine losing your whole family, and then finding out that you were supposed to die with them!"

"I guess she's tougher than she looks," replied Billy. "We still haven't figured out what we're going to do with her."

"Billy! You make her sound like just another one of Father's trinkets," Gwyneth scolded.

"I'm sorry, Gwyn. I didn't mean it that way. I just don't know what to do."

"We'll just be her friends, Billy. That will be enough."

"I guess you're right." Inside, Billy knew she was. He thought to himself that if he were in her shoes, knowing that every time her beloved father left home he may never return, he probably wouldn't handle it as well as she could. He could also see why she became so sad every time he and his uncle had to go. Thinking of Uncle Will just then reminded him that he had not seen him all day.

"Where did your father go today, anyway?"

Gwyneth thought a moment, and then answered, "He left early, saying he was going to Liverpool to see about an estate auction that took place some time ago. He said he was trying to locate the buyer of one of the items."

"He's trying to locate one of the watches," Billy assumed.

"Does this mean you'll be leaving again?" Gwyneth asked.

"It could."

As the sun began to set behind the trees at the back of the garden, Uncle Will entered the library and placed his hat on the desk. He found Billy, Nik, Gwyneth, and Anastasia sitting around a small round table that usually stood at the end of the sofa. From the looks of things, it appeared that Billy and Nik were making a vain attempt at teaching the girls to play poker. No sooner had he entered than Aunt Catherine appeared, carrying a piece of very ornate paper. They greeted each other with a kiss; and then Aunt Catherine asked for everyone's attention.

"Listen, everybody. We've been invited to spend tomorrow evening at the home of Geoffrey and Clara Radcliffe. They are having a party to celebrate the engagement of their daughter Mary to Mr. Alfred Peele. William, I took the liberty of accepting. I hope you don't mind."

"Not at all," he replied, noting the look of enthusiastic anticipation on the faces of both Catherine and Gwyneth. "I take it you boys would like to go; and Anastasia, we'd be honored if you would join us."

"Oh, do come with us, Anastasia," Gwyneth pleaded. "You'll have such a wonderful time. There will be music and dancing and... Well, you'll see. The Radcliffes always have the nicest parties!"

Billy sat absently shuffling the cards. He glanced at Nik, who seemed to be waiting for him to respond first. They shrugged at each other and then nodded. Billy spoke up.

"Sure. Sounds like fun."

Later, when everyone had retired to their rooms following dinner, Billy found Aunt Catherine sitting alone in the library, reading a book. The flickering light of the single lamp cast pulsating shadows around the room. The only sound, other than that of his footsteps, was the sound of the grandfather clock.

"Aunt Catherine?"

She looked up and removed the thin wire-framed glasses she was wearing. She could see the hesitation in his face.

"What is it, Billy?"

"It's about tomorrow night."

"The party?" she ventured.

For a response, Billy looked at his feet and thrust his hands into his pockets.

"I want to dance with Anastasia," he whispered, as if terrified that someone else might hear him, "but I don't know how. I'm afraid I'll step on her toes or something and end up looking like an idiot and..."

Aunt Catherine giggled softly, put down her book, and stood up. "And you want me to teach you."

"Could you?"

"Billy, I would love to." With that, she gestured for him to come closer. He nervously placed one arm around her waist and took her hand in his. His nervousness was compounded by the fact that she was a bit taller than he was, making it all the more awkward. It didn't take long for him to do exactly what he was afraid of doing and step on Aunt Catherine's toes. She took it in stride, laughing it off as they turned around the floor. She counted off the beats to make up for the fact that there was no music, stopping often to remind her anxious nephew to relax.

As they continued, Billy asked, "Are you really my aunt?"

"Of course I am, Billy," Aunt Catherine answered. "I married your uncle, didn't I?"

"Yeah, but..." Billy struggled to respond. He started to lose his place and stepped on her toes again.

"Billy, you needn't worry about such things."

"How did you meet him?" he asked.

Aunt Catherine laughed. "Believe it or not, I met him in 1939."

"1939?!"

"Yes, I forgot that he never bothered to tell you," she continued. "It was during the war, World War Two that is. He was living near the farm where I grew up. I was living with my aunt and uncle, because my parents thought it was safer than living in London at the time."

Billy interrupted, "What was he doing in England?"

"I wasn't sure at the time. He wouldn't really talk about it. Eventually, though, he told me about the watch."

"What did you say?"

Aunt Catherine smiled, "I thought he was mad. All that time, I thought that I had finally met a truly kind and decent man. He was so different from the rest of the Americans in our town. Then he comes out with this watch nonsense. What's a girl to do?"

"Then what happened?"

"He showed me that it was true. Soon after the war, all the other Americans went home, but he stayed. He asked me to marry him. When I told him I had always dreamt of having a Victorian wedding, I never imagined that it would be so authentic. We decided to stay here."

"But, what about your parents?"

Aunt Catherine paused, and then drew a deep breath. "My parents were killed during the bombing of London. At that point, I really had no reason to stay."

"I'm sorry," Billy said. He stepped on her toes again.

The lesson progressed at a disjointed pace until they were interrupted by the sound of a single pair of hands slowly clapping. Billy wheeled around in a panic and saw Uncle Will grinning at him.

"Really cutting the rug there, boy," he chuckled. "Don't stop on my account."

Billy glared at him in response.

"William, you're simply jealous," Aunt Catherine said, turning away from him in mock aloofness.

"I sure am," he replied. "If only I were that good. He winked at his wife and turned to Billy. "Relax. Your secret's safe with me."

The following evening, everyone climbed aboard a large, black, horse-drawn coach for the short ride to the Radcliffe home. The sprawling estate stood just a few miles from the Sheppard house, which was very small in comparison. Huge brass lamps illuminated its marble facade. Shimmering lace curtains hung in the tall windows. In front of the house, a large courtyard was centered on a fountain. At the center of the fountain stood a statue of the Greek god Hermes, which usually represented commerce. It was appropriate, since Geoffrey Radcliffe, the master of the estate, was a prominent businessman. As numerous coaches and hansom carriages arrived at the front door, footmen assisted the passengers to the steps.

Once there, the guests were greeted by Mr. and Mrs. Radcliffe. Mr. Radcliffe was a very large man, whose vest looked as if it was about to burst open. A gold watch chain swung wildly from the pocket. What little hair he had was jet black, and an equally black mustache completely covered his mouth. Mrs. Radcliffe was as thin and frail as her husband was fat. She wore a dark blue dress that was covered in lace. Next to them stood the newly engaged couple, Mary Radcliffe and Alfred Peele. Mary was an exact copy of her frail mother, except for her mother's gray hair. Her fiancé, Mr. Peele, was gangly and bucktoothed, with ears that stuck straight out from the sides of his head. The two of them giggled incessantly as well wishers passed by. Billy and Nik had to struggle to keep from laughing out loud.

As Mr. Radcliffe greeted Uncle Will, his booming voice seemed to overpower every other sound.

"Sheppard! Good to see you old boy!" He reached down and gave his watch chain a tug, removing a large, jewel encrusted, gold watch from his vest pocket. Billy's eyes lit up at the sight of it. "I finally got 'round to finding a suitable chain for the watch you gave me for my birthday!"

Uncle Will examined it. "I take it the watch is still keeping good time."

Mr. Radcliffe held it up, and Uncle Will took *Tempus Fugit* from his vest pocket. They compared the two, making small talk about the accuracy of the pieces. Mr. Radcliffe suddenly noticed Billy and Nik standing nearby. Uncle Will made brief introductions. Billy put out his hand and nearly winced at the crushing force of his host's vigorous handshake.

Uncle Will and the boys continued up the wide marble steps leading into the house. Billy sidled up to his uncle, shaking the cramp from his fingers.

"That was some watch," he whispered. "Are you sure he's not a member of..."

Uncle Will interrupted with a laugh. "Good heavens, no! Could you imagine him keeping quiet about anything?" The words had hardly left Uncle Will's mouth when Radcliffe's thunderous voice was heard again, greeting another guest, drowning out all other conversation.

The guests were directed into a large hall just off the foyer. To Billy, the room seemed as big as the gymnasium at his high school. At the far end, a small orchestra played a waltz as guests who had already arrived were milling about, greeting one another. Butlers circulated between the guests, carrying trays of small glasses of punch. Billy and Nik stuck close together, afraid of doing something that might offend their hosts or the other guests. They soon observed a number of guests approaching the center of the room as the orchestra began a new selection. Aunt Catherine leaned toward Billy.

"Here's your chance," she whispered in his ear, pointing discretely toward Anastasia.

Anastasia was standing next to Gwyneth, looking out across the room. She was wearing a burgundy dress that Aunt Catherine had given her for the occasion. The pointed toes of her black, laced shoes were barely visible under the hem of the skirt. Around her shoulders, she had draped a black lace shawl. Her light hair was tied up in curls. For the first time in quite a while, Billy thought, she actually looked like royalty.

She didn't seem to think so, as she kept self-consciously putting her hand over the scar on her left cheek. From where the boys were standing, it looked like Gwyneth was trying to convince her not to worry about it. They decided to intervene.

"What's up?" Billy asked nonchalantly.

"Oh, Billy," Gwyneth said, "I tried to tell her that it's barely noticeable, but she'll have none of it."

"What is barely noticeable?" Nik asked.

Anastasia answered by covering the scar with her hand and looking sheepishly at the ground.

"I don't see anything," Billy said, deliberately staring right at her. "Do you see anything, Nik?"

"I see nothing."

Anastasia reluctantly lowered her hand and cracked a faint smile. She glanced at Billy.

"Would you like to dance?" he asked, putting out his hand.

Much to Billy's relief, she accepted; and the two were out on the floor. Billy was awkward at first, but managed not to step on her toes.

As they turned, he could see Nik rolling his eyes in exasperation. He also saw, with some relief, Aunt Catherine nodding her approval. Billy looked nervously into Anastasia's eyes; and she smiled coyly. For a few minutes, they said nothing to each other. Billy finally spoke up.

"You'll have to bear with me. I'm new at this." He smirked at his own clumsiness.

"You are doing fine," she answered in her Russian accent.

"You look nice this evening." Come on, Billy, he thought to himself, you can do better than that.

"Thank you."

As they continued to dance, Billy's thoughts raced as he tried to come up with something intelligent to say to her. The more he thought about it, the less he was sure if he even had anything to say. While he certainly found her attractive, he wasn't sure if he had any real feelings for her beyond that. He also considered the fact that Nik had much more in common with her, especially since he was also Russian. He dreaded the thought of her coming between them. It was becoming obvious that a friendly rivalry was already forming because of her. As he considered these things, he barely noticed when the music ended. They and the other couples applauded politely. As the orchestra got ready to play another selection, Nik appeared at Billy's side.

"May I?" He gestured toward Anastasia, eyeing Billy with a look of mild jealousy. Billy simply stepped back and smiled, giving Nik the same look. Just as Anastasia floated away with her new partner, Billy slipped to the edge of the room and found a few empty chairs. As soon as he sat down, Gwyneth appeared and sat down next to him. She noticed how he was looking at Nik and Anastasia.

"Billy, what's the matter?"

"Oh, nothing," he answered, folding his arms. "I was just thinking how cool it would be if I spoke Russian. I'd probably have *so* much more to talk about!" He rolled his eyes in disgust.

"Billy," Gwyneth responded, "are you jealous?!"

He blurted out in exasperation, "Just look at them! She's obviously having more fun now than she was having a minute ago! Now, I guess I'll end up spending the rest of the evening parked on this chair."

"Well," Gwyneth answered, "you could ask me to dance with you."

"Oh, swell! He gets to dance with the princess, and I get to dance with my cousin!"

Gwyneth shot back, "What are you talking about? If you want to spend the evening moping, you've no one to blame but yourself."

Billy paused for a moment. Scanning the room, he could easily see that he was the only one not having a good time.

"Okay, Gwyn," he relented, "would you like to dance?"

"I would be honored to dance with you."

After a brief turn around the floor with Gwyneth, Billy strolled around the perimeter of the room, nodding politely to the other guests he encountered along the way. He spent most of his walk admiring the paintings and tapestries that decorated the room. He became so engrossed that he barely noticed the passage of time. Eventually, he came to the far end of the hall, opposite the orchestra. There, a large set of glass doors framed by heavy curtains opened onto a wide stone porch. The cool night air filled his lungs and snapped him to attention.

Looking through the doorway, he made out the silhouette of someone standing at the railing, facing into the darkness. Stepping onto the porch, he paused to let his eyes adjust, and recognized Anastasia. Coming to her side, he could see that she had been crying.

"You all right?" he asked awkwardly.

She turned to him, her eyes glistening in the light from inside the doors. She twisted the corner of her shawl around her finger.

"I was just thinking. Tonight reminded me of the parties we have at the Winter Palace. My sisters and I..." She hung her head and swallowed hard.

"Anastasia?" Billy wasn't sure what to say. He reached down and took her hand.

"I miss them," she continued hesitatingly. "Sometimes, I find myself thinking they are still alive. That they are looking for me. But, that is not possible, is it?"

Billy's mind raced for something to tell her. He felt like he was completely blowing it again. The look in her eyes told him she knew he didn't have any answers, but that same look told him it didn't matter.

She took a deep breath and cracked a smile.

"If Olga were here, she would tell me to stop being such a baby."

"Olga?"

"My eldest sister. She was always so—how do you say—proper. I used to love playing jokes on her." She sighed again, shifting her eyes. Billy's fingers intertwined with hers. "I have no one to play jokes on now."

Billy looked out into the darkness. After a long wait, he gave Anastasia's hand a gentle squeeze.

"You've got me." It sounded like a question.

Anastasia turned to face Billy. "Why did you come for me?"

"Oh, I was just wandering around the place, and I saw you standing out here, so..."

"No," she interrupted, "Why did you come to Russia?"

The question left Billy standing open-mouthed. Up to now, he never gave the matter any thought. He recalled how his uncle had scolded him for his recklessness. All he could say was, "I don't know. I guess we...I guess I..."

She looked into his eyes, and he tried hard not to look away. Still holding her hand he drew her closer. It seemed for a moment that they forgot what they were just talking about. With his other hand,

Billy reached up to her face and brushed aside a lock of hair, revealing the scar on her cheek; but he took no notice of it. She closed her eyes as he moved closer. The sound of the party seemed to fade away. Billy closed his eyes.

"Billy! There you are!" Nik's voice crashed through Billy's ears like a bull through a china shop! Billy's eyes popped open to see Anastasia startle and step back, turning away toward the railing. For the briefest moment, Billy thought he saw her suppressing laughter. He turned and glared at a smiling Nik.

Nik continued, "Your uncle was wondering where you had gone. He said it is time to go."

"Thanks, Nik," Billy said coldly. The thought of throwing his friend over the railing flashed across his mind.

"What?" Nik was playing dumb. He turned to leave. Anastasia followed, quickly glancing over her shoulder. As Billy started to follow, she suddenly stopped and looked at him. He studied the mischievous look on her face; but before he could tell what she was up to, she leaned toward him and gave him a gentle peck on the cheek. With that, she turned and walked briskly across the hall to where Uncle Will and the rest were waiting.

Once they arrived home, everyone moved to the library, where Uncle Will started a roaring fire in the fireplace. He then sat at his desk, winding the watch. Billy and Nik sat on the sofa. Aunt Catherine sat in her usual spot, working on her cross-stitch, while Gwyneth and Anastasia playfully improvised at the piano.

"Gentlemen," Uncle Will addressed the boys, "I need to brief you on what our next move is." This brought the boys eagerly to the edge of the sofa. "We need to return to the workshop. I found out that the Michael Redgrave who purchased Maybrick's watch, Tempus Omnia Relevat, sold it at auction. Now as we know, he was ignorant of the watch's properties. We need to find out what happened to it. The information we need can best be found back in the workshop."

"How?" asked Billy.

"I'm not sure yet. I have some fairly extensive files on the antique watch market. I'll think of something," Uncle Will answered. "Anastasia, you are welcome to join us, if you feel up to it. Otherwise, you may stay here. My wife and daughter will look after you."

The grand duchess looked back and forth at the two boys, who were grinning expectantly. A much-welcomed smile came to her face.

"I think I would like to come with you," she answered in stilted English.

Uncle Will nodded. "Understand, Anastasia, that your identity must never be revealed at any time or any place. You must never go anywhere without one of us; and you should let us do most of the talking should anyone ask you who you are. I realize that the events of the past weeks have been very hard on you both emotionally and psychologically; but it is very important that you follow my instructions to the letter. Is that understood?"

She looked at him quizzically, as if not completely understanding him. Nik noticed this and spoke to her in Russian. She then nodded.

"I understand."

"Good. We'll leave in the morning."

The morning sun shone through the massive windows of the library. A light mist still hugged the ground outside. Uncle Will stood in front of his desk, fidgeting impatiently as Aunt Catherine adjusted his tie for him.

"William, I don't care where you're going. I will not have you leaving the house looking unkempt."

The four young people stood in a circle at the center of the room, joining hands and bowing their heads. Gwyneth insisted that they not leave until she could pray for their safety. Having done that, she embraced each of them and said 'good-bye.' Uncle Will took the watch from his vest pocket, gave the stem a few turns to ensure it was running, flipped open the cover, set it, and pointed it toward the rising sun. By now, the boys hardly reacted when the large black hole opened before them. Time travel was becoming as commonplace to them as an airplane ride to a traveling salesman.

The same could not be said, however, for Anastasia. She gasped loudly, clutching Billy's arm with almost painful force, and crossing herself with the other hand. He had to quickly put his arm around her to keep her from collapsing to the floor. Uncle Will and Billy paused and studied her terrified face. Nik spoke to her once again in Russian. From his tone, the others could tell he was trying to reassure her. Billy stepped forward, taking her free hand.

"It's okay. We do this all the time. How do you think you got here?"

She pulled her hand away, glaring at him. Uncle Will approached her and looked squarely into her blue eyes.

"Anastasia. Trust me."

Uncle Will turned and walked through the hole. The boys, flanking Anastasia on either side, escorted her through it.

Chapter Seventeen

They arrived in the workshop, finding it exactly as it was the moment they left it. The boys quickly ushered Anastasia to a chair. Her eyes darted wildly about the room, trying to take it all in at once. Almost immediately, she spotted her Kodak Brownie sitting on the workbench.

"My camera!" She dashed across the room, scooping it up and holding it close to her. After a moment, she examined it carefully, noticing that it still had the original role of film in it.

"Billy, Nik, I would like very much to take your picture again. You also, Mr. Sheppard. I want a photograph of the men who saved my life."

The three hastily shuffled into a pose and smiled; and she snapped the picture. Then, they all took seats at the table. Before any of them could speak another word, there was a knock at the heavy wooden door that separated the workshop from the rest of the basement. The knocking was followed by the voice of Carolyn.

"Billy," she called. The sound of her voice froze everyone in the room. Billy glanced at the door. Thank God it was still locked, he thought.

His mother continued, "Billy, are you in there? I have something for you."

Billy turned to the others to see that Uncle Will was already in the process of stealthily ushering them into the steel cabinet. As he closed the cabinet, he gestured to Billy to go ahead and open the door. Billy approached the door. Suddenly, he realized that he was still dressed for 1889. He spun around and frantically scanned the room, trying to find his own clothes. Carolyn continued to call to him.

"Coming, mom!" Billy replied, as he spotted his clothes in a heap in the corner. Limbs and garments flying, he threw off the old shirt, exposing the faded T-shirt he had on under it. He then pulled his jeans on over the brown wool trousers, and dashed to the door to unlatch the bolt.

"Yes, Mom?"

"Here's a package for Uncle Will. You can put it with the rest of his mail," she answered, handing him a small brown box and glancing apprehensively over Billy's shoulder. "What's going on in here?"

"Nothing," Billy quipped, thinking of his uncle and friends crammed uncomfortably in the steel tool cabinet behind him. "I'm just cleaning up."

"Well, don't get too dirty. We'll be eating dinner soon."

"Don't worry, I won't."

Carolyn smiled and stepped through the door into the workshop, her eyes passing over the room.

"You've cleaned it up quite a bit," she remarked. "Your uncle will probably have a fit. That's why he rarely lets me in here." She moved toward the table. Please don't sit down, Billy thought as he followed her closely. That was exactly what she did; taking the chair that placed her with her back to the tool cabinet.

"I remember when he first moved in with us," she began. "You we're just starting school. I had planned on making this a sewing room for your sister and myself." She continued to reminisce, but Billy hardly heard a word of it. He could feel the heat rising from his own body, as the wool trousers under his jeans began to itch. As he stood facing his mother, he could see the door of the cabinet slowing inching open. The hair stood on the back of his neck when he saw Uncle Will stick his head out of the door. Carolyn was still talking, completely oblivious to her brother's presence. Uncle Will could see this, as well as Billy's stiff expression, and began to make the most ridiculous faces at her. It was all Billy could do to contain himself; half of him wanted to laugh out loud, the other half wanted to kill the man in the tool cabinet. With his eyes, he begged his uncle to stop, hoping his mother wouldn't notice. He decided to cut his mother's visit short. He held the workshop door open.

"I'll be finished in just a few minutes, Mom."

"Okay, but just a few more minutes."

With that, Carolyn stood up, and then turned to leave. Billy closed and latched the door behind her. He placed an ear to the door to hear her return upstairs, closing the basement door behind her. He heaved a sigh of extreme relief, and slumped into one of the chairs.

"You can come out now, guys."

The cabinet door sprang open, and three equally relieved people spilled out.

"That was too close," said Uncle Will, taking the box from Billy, who was already holding it in the air, glaring coldly at him. He studied the box, which looked soiled with age, then tore it open. He reached inside and recovered a small flat spool of thin steel wire.

"What is it?" asked Billy.

"It's a recording wire," replied Uncle Will, unwinding a bit of the loose end. The shiny metal wire was hardly thicker than sewing thread. "This was used in the days before tape. There's sound recorded on here."

"Of what?" Nik asked.

"I don't know. I'm trying to think of who would have sent it to me."

The three young people stood motionless, watching Uncle Will study the spool in his hand, as if trying to coax the answer out of it. Suddenly, he blurted out, "Marcus!"

"Marcus sent it to you?" Billy asked.

"He's the only other person I know who had a wire recorder."

"The only *other* person?"

In response to Billy's question, Uncle Will handed him the wire, dashed to the workbench, and began to rummage through the piles of junk and parts on the shelf below it. After a few noisy moments, he reached as far back as his arms would allow and produced a large black box. It was dirty, with marred corners, and had a cover held in place by rusted latches. He lifted it to the top of the workbench with a loud grunt, raising a plume of dust. Unlatching the lid revealed the machine inside. It was slightly larger than a toaster, with an art deco design. Its controls were sparse, and a loudspeaker was situated in the center of the front panel. Uncle Will carefully lifted the device out of its case and placed it on the bench. Billy, Nik, and Anastasia watched in amazement as he took the spool of wire and threaded it onto the machine. Once it was threaded, Uncle Will threw the switch. Contrary to everyone's expectations, nothing happened. Uncle Will stood scratching his beard. He tried the switch again, to no avail; then he leaned over the machine and placed his ear against the side of it.

"Ah-ha," he said. With that he reached for a screwdriver and began to remove the cover from the machine as the young people watched intently. He opened the recorder to reveal the primitive electronics inside. It was a jumble of old wire and components. On one side of the steel chassis, there were fixed a few old vacuum tubes. All but one of them were glowing a dull orange.

"Just what I suspected," Uncle Will announced. "We've got a bad tube." He spun around and headed for a box in the corner. Digging through it, and creating another huge cloud of dust in the process, he produced a replacement. After a few more moments of tinkering, the wire recorder hummed to life. Billy, Nik, and Anastasia all looked at it with wonder, which gave Uncle Will quite a chuckle.

"What's so funny?" asked Billy.

"You kids! It's ironic how all of you are so fascinated by this thing. To you boys, it's an antique; but to Anastasia, it's a glimpse of the future! You're all just as fascinated, but for different reasons. Now, let's hear what it has to say."

Uncle Will flipped the switch once again, and the machine began to play back the wire. It made a crackling noise not unlike that of a scratchy phonograph record. Soon, the crackling was accompanied by a man's voice. Uncle Will and the boys immediately recognized it at the voice of Dr. Janus. He seemed to be dictating some sort of medical information, using the wire recorder for transcription. His voice droned on for about a minute when it was interrupted mid-sentence by a short thump. Then a new voice was heard.

"William," the voice said with a British accent, "Marcus here. I don't have much time, so I'll be brief. I can only hope this reaches you in time. If you're listening to it, that means I'm either dead or most certainly incapacitated. And you may thank the good Dr. Janus for it."

Billy had difficulty believing that the voice was Marcus'. He couldn't connect the distinguished, lilting voice on the wire with the shriveled lunatic at Briarcliff Asylum. The voice continued.

"He's hell-bent on getting his hands on every one of the watches. I found out about Maybrick. The man he sold it to auctioned it off! Truth be told, I bought it! To keep Janus away from it, I gave it to that old Dutch watchmaker, Casper Ten Boom. You remember him; the one with the great white beard, looked like Father Christmas. I met him in Amsterdam, at the Naval Observatory. Near as I can tell, the old man still has it. Janus has caught up with me. I'm sorry, William, I'm afraid he's got me right where he wants me. I hope better things for you. He's on his way here even now."

Marcus' voice was followed by the faint sound of footsteps, then by a strange squeal. Then, suddenly, the spool ran out of wire. Uncle Will stood in silence, staring blankly at the spinning take-up reel. Billy reached over and shut off the machine.

"Okay, Uncle Will, now what?"

"For now," Uncle Will began, without looking up, "I need to check some of my old files, provided you haven't thrown them out in the mad fit of cleaning you had down here."

Billy raised his hands in surrender, much the way his uncle often did.

"I didn't throw anything away! It's all in those boxes under the workbench!"

"Probably messed up my whole filing system," Uncle Will mumbled, eyeing Billy with mock suspicion. "I'll be a while. Why don't you two show our guest around downstairs?"

Billy followed his uncle's instructions by bringing Anastasia down to the vault, with Nik, to see all of the artifacts stored there. She was just as astonished by the enormous collection of clothes, documents, jewelry, and the like as she was by the workshop above. She took a flowing ball gown from the rack and held it in front of her, gasping with delight. Billy and Nik looked on with great satisfaction. She'd make one heck of a prom date, Billy thought to himself, remembering the party at the Radcliffe house. He imagined the difficulty of explaining to everyone where he'd met her. As they continued their tour of the vault, they could occasionally hear the voice of Uncle Will, muttering incessantly as he rifled through his papers. They had nearly lost track of how long they were down there, when Uncle Will's voice could be heard once again, shouting down to them.

"Kids! I think I found it!"

They rushed to the ladder to find Uncle Will on his way down. He reached the bottom, out of breath.

"What did you find," Billy asked, "the other watch?"

"I think," Uncle Will wheezed. "I found the address in Holland of the watchmaker Marcus mentioned."

"So that's where we're going next?" Nik asked.

Uncle Will answered, "It's all we have to go on at this point. We'd better get dressed."

With that, Uncle Will began rummaging through the racks of clothes, looking for what they would need. He handed the boys two suits comprising of neatly pressed trousers and matching jackets. He also gave them two pairs of black leather shoes. For himself, he found a dark pinstriped, three-piece suit. For Anastasia, he took out a blue jacket and knee-length skirt with a white blouse. When he handed it to her, he was not completely prepared for her reaction.

"I am not wearing that, Mr. Sheppard."

"Why not?"

She didn't respond right away. She stood staring at the outfit with a look of disdain. She muttered something in Russian.

"What?" Billy asked, looking at Nik.

"She thinks it's too revealing. She says she can't believe anyone would go out in public dressed like that."

"Anastasia," said Uncle Will, "please understand that this is what a lot of women in the 1940's wear." He took the skirt and held it in front of her. It was likely tailored for someone Aunt Catherine's height, so the skirt was longer on Anastasia. "See that. It covers your knees."

Anastasia was not impressed with this fact. She folded her arms and stood straight up, glaring defiantly at Uncle Will.

"Okay, fine then," he said, tossing the outfit aside, "let's see what else we have."

After a few moments of rummaging through the racks, he found a dress for her that nearly reached the floor, but was still likely to pass for normal for the time period for which they were bound. She reluctantly accepted it. Uncle Will ushered the boys back up to the workshop to give her some privacy.

Billy and Nik stood at the workbench, carefully studying the wire recorder as they waited for Anastasia. Their attention was abruptly redirected when they heard the characteristic snap of a handgun's loading mechanism. They wheeled around and saw Uncle Will holding a .45 caliber automatic pistol, which he promptly put inside his jacket.

"I'm not taking any chances," he said.

"Just what are we planning to do in Holland anyway, start a war?" Billy asked with a horrified expression.

Uncle Will chuckled, "We won't need to. In the Europe of 1944, there's enough of that to go around."

"Do you think we'll run into Janus there?" asked Nik.

"Let's hope not," replied Uncle Will.

Billy thought aloud for a moment, "So we have one watch, we know another one was destroyed, and Janus has at least one; so we need to get the one in Holland before he does. That leaves just one problem."

"How do we get the one he has away from him?" Uncle Will completed the thought.

"Right," Billy and Nik said together.

"We'll have to cross that bridge when we come to it."

At that moment, the conversation was interrupted by the appearance of Anastasia, wearing the long dress Uncle Will gave her. Her expression was much warmer than before.

"How do I look?" she asked, spinning slowly.

"Fine," Uncle Will said absently, taking the watch from his pocket. "I've already made the orbital displacement calculations, so we can get going." He held the watch in front of the shaft of sunlight coming through the window.

Chapter Eighteen

They arrived in Haarlem, Holland in the middle of the night, which was fortunate; since the sight of four people suddenly appearing in the middle of the street was bound to attract unwanted attention. They made their way into a nearby alley to get their bearings. Uncle Will directed them behind a large trash bin to conceal them from anyone who might pass along the sidewalk. Anastasia, still a bit shaky from her injuries, clutched Billy's arm tightly with a combination of fear and cold, as the stiff March air rushed by. They all fell silent at the sound of approaching footsteps. As the footsteps grew louder, they became unmistakable as the sound of leather boots. Uncle Will drew his handgun and carefully peered around the side of the trash bin. The figure crossing the alley bore the characteristic outline of a German Gestapo officer. He passed by without stopping, without even turning his head. As the footsteps faded, Uncle Will let out a quiet breath in relief, which was echoed by the others. They waited a few minutes before exiting the alley.

Once they reached the street, Uncle Will pointed toward the east, where the sky was beginning to take on a faint glow.

"The sun will be up pretty soon. We'd better hurry."

"Where do we have to go?" asked Billy.

"To the watch shop on the Barteljorisstraat," his uncle replied, taking a small slip of paper out of his pocket. Billy noticed that Uncle Will had scribbled a crude map on the paper, showing the route to the shop. They all headed in the direction the map indicated.

By the time they reached the shop, the sun was above the horizon. A few people walked along the street some distance away, the first of many people who would be traveling this usually busy shopping street. The shop was set into the first floor of a narrow three-story building. The large glass front window bore the words *"Ten Boom—Horloges."* Uncle Will put his face to the window, cupping his hands around his eyes. His expression sank.

"I think we may be too late."

Billy and Nik were too busy studying the name on the window to digest what he said. Billy thought he had heard that name before.

Suddenly, it occurred to him.

"Uncle Will," he began, "the name on the window. Should I know that name?"

Uncle Will stood back from the glass and replied, "That all depends, boy."

Billy searched his memory for the name, trying to recall where he had heard it before. Just then, he recalled several years ago, his grandmother reading him a story called "The Hiding Place," about Corrie Ten Boom and her family, and how they rescued Jews from the Nazis by hiding them in a secret room in the back of the house. His eyes widened as he realized that he stood in front of the very place. He looked at his uncle, who responded with his usual knowing smile.

"You..." Billy started, "you knew Corrie Ten Boom?!"

Uncle Will answered, "Well, I've never actually met her, no. And I've only had a few brief encounters with her father. I don't really know them personally; but I'm well acquainted with who they are."

At that moment, there was a lull in the traffic on the Barteljorisstraat. Uncle Will seized on the opportunity. He gestured to the young people to wait, as he made his way down a nearby alley that led to the side of the house. Billy and Nik looked at each other, both wondering what Uncle Will was up to. Anastasia studied their faces with more than a little concern.

"Billy, who are these people your uncle speaks of?" she asked.

"They were a family of Christians who hid Jews from the Nazis. They got caught and sent to a concentration camp..." His answer was interrupted by a stern glance from Nik, who was now standing directly behind her. Billy suddenly realized that Anastasia had no idea who the Nazis were, let alone anything about concentration camps. He also remembered the warning he had gotten from his uncle about being careful not to reveal certain things to her for that very reason. She turned and looked at Nik.

"What is wrong?"

Nik hesitated, and then answered, "It's a long, complicated story; and I'm afraid we don't have the time to tell it." With great relief, he looked up to see Uncle Will opening the shop door from the inside, and waving them in off the street. He gestured for Anastasia to go in ahead of him. Billy came up behind him.

"Good catch," he whispered.

The group entered the deserted watch shop. From the look of things, its previous occupants had left unexpectedly, especially in light of the fact that Uncle Will had very little trouble gaining entry. It had been abandoned for some time, as evidenced by a thin layer of dust on everything in the room. Also, none of the clocks on display in the shop were running. Nik nudged Billy and pointed to the floor near a doorway that led to the rest of the house. Billy stifled a gasp as he noticed a small blood stain on the wood. Uncle Will was slowly scanning the glass display cases, looking at the watches that still remained inside. After making a circuit of the room, he paused to think.

"We must be too late," he thought aloud. "You kids wait here. I'm going to scout around for a minute to find out if anyone around here knows anything. I'll be right back, so sit tight." With that, he stepped out the door and walked up the street. The young people stood looking at each other for a moment, then resigned themselves to wait. Anastasia immediately took the opportunity to sit on a nearby stool. Nik made his way to the window and scanned the street outside. Suddenly, the sight of a group of three Nazi officers moving along the sidewalk toward the shop caught his attention. They were far enough away that Nik could safely withdraw from the window without being noticed. He grabbed Billy by the arm, interrupting his browsing through the display cases.

"I think we have trouble coming."

Billy confirmed this by having his own look out the window. By now he could see that two of them wore the same uniform as the Gestapo officer they had seen in the alley. The third man was dressed in the black uniform with red swastika armband of the Nazi Schutzstaffel, the SS. He dashed toward the counter at the back of the shop.

"Hide!" he said, gesturing wildly to the others. They all ran through the doorway into the workroom. From there, they passed through another doorway at the back of the room to find a winding staircase leading upstairs. Once they reached the second floor, they ran through a small sitting room, passing through another door to reach a bedroom at the front of the house. Two windows looked out over the street. Billy slipped across the room and dropped to his knees in front of one of the windows. He carefully peered through the lace curtain just in time to see the three Nazis approach the entrance to the watch shop. As he ducked away from the window, he gestured for Nik to go back the way he came in. Then, all three of them met in the corridor at the top of the stairs.

Scrambling through another doorway they found themselves in a room at the back of the house. Once inside the room, Billy searched for cover. Peering into an open closet, he saw an opening in the wall. It was the secret compartment where so many others on the run from the Nazis had sought refuge.

"There!"

Immediately, all three were crouching into the low, dark room behind the closet. Billy slid the section of wall that served as a door into place. They huddled together in perfect darkness, waiting. Billy felt Anastasia's hand around his arm, her head pressed hard against his shoulder.

Billy thought this hiding place had worked for so many others; perhaps it would work for them. At once, his thoughts were interrupted by the sound of footsteps downstairs. He and the others fell silent as they waited for the soldiers to leave. The heat in the chamber was already stifling. Soon, the footsteps could be heard on the stairs, then silence. Billy's eyes stung as sweat trickled into them. He could feel Anastasia trembling next to him. The silence was broken by the sound of the door opening, followed by the sound of boots on the wooden floor, followed by a much heavier silence. The sound of his own blood rushing through his head became deafening as Billy prayed desperately for the men to leave. He wondered where his uncle was. The oppressive silence was again broken by a voice.

"You may come out now," it said with a pronounced German accent. "We know you are here."

Billy had the fleeting notion that he had heard the voice before. The three stayed motionless, as if hoping to bluff their way out of this mess. Footsteps approached even closer until they stopped just beyond the false wall. Billy could hear the creak of leather boots, so close they sounded like they were inside the chamber with him.

The voice continued, "We have been aware of this secret room for some time. My patience is running out. Open the door!"

At that moment, something odd occurred to Billy. Why was this man speaking to them in English? Weren't they in Holland? He couldn't stand it anymore. He felt like a mortally wounded mouse being batted around by a cat. He slowly turned his head, slid the board aside, and ventured a look. His eyes widened in terror as he recognized the face of Dr. Janus, grinning at him with obvious satisfaction. He was the man in the black uniform, his hat bearing the Death's head emblem of the SS. Billy felt a wave of nausea race through his body.

"What ever are you hiding from, young man?" Janus asked. Slowly, the three young people began to emerge from their grossly inadequate hiding place. The other two soldiers leveled Schmeizer sub-machine guns at them, waving their prisoners out into the corridor. They were unceremoniously shoved across the room to the stairs and down to the workshop. Anastasia was nearly sent tumbling down the steps. Once everyone reached the watch shop, the three captives were lined up in front of a glass display case. Janus began to pace the floor before them, studying their faces carefully. He stopped in front of Billy.

"The watch. I want it."

"But I don't..." Billy failed to get out another word as Janus' open hand slammed across his cheek. The force of the blow nearly knocked him over. Anastasia gasped loudly.

"You know very well where it is," Janus hissed. "Now tell me!"

"I said I don't..." Another blow landed on Billy's still throbbing face. He could feel a lump forming in his throat as he tried desperately not to cry out. His fists clenched tightly.

Janus continued, "I doubt very much whether your demented uncle would leave you and your time traveling friends to your own devices in such a place. Perhaps he is here also."

"He left," Billy replied. "I don't know where..." He was again interrupted by Janus' raised hand. He flinched, but no blow came. Janus merely rolled his eyes.

"Yes, yes, so you keep saying. You don't know. Of course not." Janus moved in front of Anastasia, who eyed him very nervously. "Her Imperial Highness, Grand Duchess Anastasia, I presume."

She looked back and forth at the two boys, who were also glancing at each other in bewilderment.

"I wonder, Anastasia," Janus purred, "why these brave young men only managed to save you from the Bolsheviks and left your dear family to die."

"What are you talking about?" Nik asked.

Janus stepped toe to toe with Nik. "It's ironic, really. You had the power to save all the Romanovs, but you didn't use it." Janus took a few steps back and folded his arms.

"What is he talking about, Nikolai?" asked Anastasia. "What does he mean?"

Nik's face was turning red as his bottom lip began to quiver. Billy was equally horrified.

"Billy?" Anastasia's voice was cracking.

"What I am talking about, fair Anastasia," Janus explained, "is a piece of history!"

She grabbed Nik's arm and looked straight into his eyes. "What does he mean?!"

"I'll tell you what I mean," Janus said.

"No!" shouted Nik. "I will tell her." He turned back to her, lowered his gaze, and drew a deep breath. "We were able to rescue you because we knew what would happen to you. We knew what would happen to your family too."

"Indeed, it is an historical fact even now," Janus added with a smile. "Tsar Nicholas and his family, including you my dear, were killed. These two heroic young men knew about it from recorded history, and they didn't do a thing to save the rest of them."

Anastasia stood frozen for a moment, tears flooding her eyes. All Nik could do was stand there, crushed.

"Anastasia," Billy said in a pleading tone, "we couldn't. It had already happened. You've got to understand..."

Even Billy realized how ridiculous he must have sounded to her, especially when he remembered how much she missed her family at the party.

She turned her head and glared at him with obvious pain in her eyes. Slowly, she stepped away from them, shifting her eyes to the floor. Dr. Janus broke the brief but heavy silence that followed.

"Now, where is William Sheppard?"

"I told you we don't know," Billy growled.

"Very well," replied Janus. He then turned to the two soldiers and barked an order to them in German. They responded by dashing out the door, their guns still at the ready. Once they were gone, Janus turned and approached Anastasia. Suddenly, like a rattlesnake striking its prey, he reached out and clutched her arm, causing the girl to cry out in pain. With his free hand, he reached into his jacket and withdrew a large pocket watch. Billy and Nik recoiled at the sight of it as the sunlight shining through the window reflected from its polished gold case. They could see the engraving on the cover: *Tempus Omnia Relevat*. All at once, they realized that they were indeed too late; Janus had beaten them to the watch. He knew all along that they would come there to look for it. Billy could feel hot blood flushing through his body. Janus stepped to the window and snapped the watch open. Once the dark hole had formed, he placed the watch back in his pocket, and then turned to the captive Anastasia.

"My dear little princess," he said, "you have an appointment with history."

"Where are you taking her?!" Nik screamed, lunging toward Janus. His attack was met with a quick sidestep and a severe blow to the head with the butt of Janus' Luger handgun. Nik sprawled across the floor, blood gushing from his brow. Janus leveled the gun at Billy, who by now was headed straight for him. The boys froze where they were. Anastasia struggled in vain to free herself, her face contorted by the pain of her injuries; but Janus flung her around toward the hole.

"I'm taking her back where she belongs!" Janus shouted. "July 16th, 1918!" The date instantly sent chills down the backs of Billy and Nik. Janus gave one final heave and dragged Anastasia, Grand Duchess of the Russian Empire, to be reunited with her family, and die at the hands of the Bolsheviks.

"Billy! Niko..."

The hole vanished. Both boys staggered backward in shock. Billy put out his hand to steady himself against the display case. Numbness consumed him. It was all he could do to keep from vomiting. Nik dropped to his knees with a painful wail, followed by a stream of Russian, spat through clenched teeth. Billy fought to regain his balance and made for the door in the corridor.

"Come on, we have to get out of here!"

He reached for the handle and threw open the door. The muzzle of Janus' Luger blocked his exit.

"Going somewhere?" Janus crooned. He stood alone in the alley, pocketing his watch with his other hand.

Billy stepped backward slowly. Nik rose to his feet and once again lunged at Janus, screaming in Russian. Janus merely pointed the Luger at Nik's bloody face, stopping him instantly.

"Shut up!" he barked.

"I told you we don't know where he is," whispered Billy, his eyes staring into empty space.

At that moment, the two soldiers reentered the shop. Saluting Dr. Janus with an upthrust arm, one soldier spoke to him in German. He gave them further orders. In response, one soldier stepped to the back of the shop and into the corridor that led to the rear entrance. The other soldier went into the street and waved a beckoning arm toward a truck that stood parked at the end of the street. Once the truck arrived in front of the shop, Janus gestured with his pistol for the boys to climb aboard. Armed guards wasted no time shackling their wrists and ankles. They were seated on hard wooden plank seats in the back of the truck; then the guards placed black canvas sacks over their heads. Janus climbed into the cab, next to the driver.

As the last guard climbed onto the back of the truck, he scanned the street one last time. All he saw, quite some distance down the block, was an old man in a long black coat and wide-brimmed fedora, sitting on a bench, checking the time on his gold watch.

Chapter Nineteen

If there was such a place as hell on earth, Billy would have been sure he had found it, if he could be sure of anything. At the moment, Billy was losing his mind. The last thing he could reliably remember was being bound to a chair with the canvas sack still over his head. He could hear footsteps all around him. The last voice he heard was that of Dr. Janus ordering 10cc of mescaline. It was administered in a painfully sloppy manner into his right arm, just below his elbow. It was then that he remembered the needle marks on Uncle Will's and Marcus' arms, and wondered just what this concoction would do to him. He was then cut loose from the chair and taken out of the room and down what sounded like a corridor.

A German soldier shoved him through a narrow doorway, nearly causing him to fall flat on his face. He could hear the sound of splashing as ice cold water filled his shoes. Suddenly his head was jerked backwards as the soldier pulled the sack from his head. He caught a brief glimpse of a dark stone wall in front of him; but before his eyes could fully adjust to the dim light coming from behind him, the door to his cell slammed shut, leaving him in complete darkness. The air in the room was stale and cold. The few inches of freezing water he was standing in caused his feet to ache. Within seconds, Billy was shivering.

He could hear a dull buzzing in his ears. He took a careful step forward, listening for any sound other than the rippling of water. The sound echoed around him, making it difficult to gauge the size of the room. He took another step. Where the floor should have been, his foot sank even deeper, until the water came up to his knee. The sudden drop caused Billy to fall forward, landing face first with a loud splash. The cold shocked his breath away, making it impossible to cry out. He quickly tried to right himself only to find that the entire floor was cratered and uneven, making navigation in the dark difficult at best. It became obvious that it was intended to disorient any occupants.

As the buzzing in his head grew louder, he felt as if there were insects crawling on his arms. He swatted at them furiously, shrieking in fear. The sound of his own voice was difficult to recognize. The buzzing began to break up into the sound of laughter, as if hundreds of voices were in the room with him. He flailed wildly trying to find the walls. The feeling that there were insects crawling on him had now spread to his entire body. Billy's heart was racing; his breathing was also getting faster with each passing second. When he closed his eyes, he began to see flashes of light, but when he opened his eyes, there was nothing but darkness. Soon, it didn't matter whether his eyes were opened or shut. The flashes of color became blinding in their intensity to the point that Billy began to feel sick. The water felt as if it were icy claws, clutching his legs.

After careful probing, he made his way to the wall. Running his hands over it, he could feel cold, rough stones. His opened eyes strained to find even the tiniest source of light, but there was none. Billy turned and leaned against the wall, chilled to the bone. He felt as if there was someone, or something, else in the cell with him. He lashed out at the darkness, screaming at the top of his lungs; but there was nothing. The sound of rippling water was now accented by the sound of his chattering teeth. The echoes in the room were disorienting.

In a small corner of his mind yet untouched by the drug, he wondered how Nik was holding up, assuming that he was in similar straits. Then he wondered where on earth Uncle Will was. Why hadn't he come back to the shop? Where was he now? Did he even know where they were? Soon his thoughts turned toward Anastasia. He replayed in his mind the scene in the watch shop. He wondered what he should have done differently. He shuddered when he remembered the look in her eyes. He still couldn't believe she was gone. Once again, his face began to sting where Janus had struck him, as the tears flowed into the open, bleeding cut. He wanted desperately to go home.

The fear of not being able to go home hit him even harder than when Uncle Will had reprimanded him for going back to rescue Anastasia. Up to this point, the whole thing had seemed like a very realistic game, a bit hazardous, but still fairly benign. Now the fun was over. She wasn't just part of the game, any more than he or Nik or Uncle Will was, or even Gwyneth and Aunt Catherine were. She was real. The pain was real. The blood running down his face was real.

As he grew more and more dizzy, he began to hear his own voice, even though he couldn't tell if he was consciously speaking.

"God, help me!"

He tripped and fell into the freezing puddle. As he struggled to get up, he found the wall again, and crouched down against it. Again, he could hear himself. His voice was shaky and weak. He nearly choked on the words.

"Now I lay me down to sleep.
I pray the Lord my soul to keep.

If I should die before I wake.
I pray the Lord my soul to take."

Barely a moment later, he mercifully lost consciousness.

Billy was abruptly awakened by an earsplitting screech as the door to his cell flung open. Opening his eyes to the dim light in the corridor was like staring into the sun. He raised his arm to shield them. He could barely make out the outline of a soldier filling the doorway. The soldier said something to him in German. His hesitation apparently annoyed the guard, who then stepped into the cell and shouted the exact words, this time brandishing a club. Billy raised both hands to protect himself as he scrambled to his feet. The guard took him by the arm and led him into the corridor. Billy squinted at the lights. Once they reached the end, the guard stood Billy against the wall next to a heavy steel door. Unlocking the door with a large key, the jailer opened the door, releasing a thick cloud of steam. Before Billy could comprehend it, he was thrust through the doorway into another cell. Once the door was slammed behind him, he wheeled around to see Nik sitting on the floor in one corner. Nik lifted his head, which was still bleeding, and leaped to his feet at the sight of Billy.

"Are you all right?!" they asked simultaneously, clutching each other's arms. Billy was thrilled to see his friend still alive, if not in the greatest shape. Suddenly, the atmosphere in the room had its intended effect on Billy. The air was as hot and sticky as his previous accommodations were cold. Instantly, he began to sweat profusely. The air was difficult to breathe. He could feel his knees buckling; and he dropped to the floor. Nik lowered himself to his friend's side.

"Easy, Billy. Just sit still. You will be okay."

"How long have you been in here?" asked Billy.

"Not very long. It's hard to tell. What happened to you?"

Billy shook his head. "They left me in some room filled with ice water. They gave me some kind of shot before. I'm not sure, but I'll bet it was the same stuff Janus gave to my uncle and that guy Marcus."

The two made their way to the wall and sat down. Billy was glad to be warm again, but the feeling did not last. Soon, the heaviness of the air, and the heat, which in Billy's estimation had to be far in excess of a hundred degrees, began to take their toll. Billy's head began to throb in pain. His already damp clothes clung to his sweating body, making it impossible to sit comfortably. He looked at Nik, who sat with his head hanging.

"My head is killing me," said Billy.

"Your head?" Nik retorted. "I am the one who got pistol whipped!"

"Well, it's not like I got off without a scratch," Billy replied, pointing to his swollen cheek.

"Where is that uncle of yours anyway?"

"What do you mean 'that uncle of yours?'"

"He got us into this mess!"

"Yes, thank you for stating the obvious." As annoyed as he was, Billy could easily understand Nik's frustration. Certainly, neither of them had volunteered for this. Billy thought to himself that if he had known what sort of trouble they'd be in, he would never have told Nik about the watch in the first place. Looking at Nik's oozing cut made him feel worse.

"I'm sorry about all this."

Nik forced a smile. "What are friends for?"

They sat with heads bowed for what felt like hours. Neither of them dared to move in the stifling heat. Nik began to squirm in his place.

"What are we supposed to do now?" he muttered.

"I don't know."

"How are we going to get out of here?"

"I don't know."

"How are we going to get back?"

"I DON'T KNOW!!"

Billy's shouting was answered by the opening of the cell door. The rush of cool air caused them to instinctively rush toward it. The muzzle of a Luger stopped them. The dark outline of Dr. Janus, in full Nazi SS regalia, stood before them.

"Gentlemen, surely there is no need for you to fight amongst yourselves," he said softly.

That's exactly what he wants us to do, Billy thought, realizing why they were reunited in such a place. Perhaps Janus was hoping one would turn on the other and reveal something.

"What do you want?" Billy snapped.

"You know exactly what I want. I am prepared to wait a very long time for it. You'd better hope that twisted old fool you call 'Uncle' cares enough about you to hand over the watch. Now tell me where he is."

"I already told you..."

"Enough!" Janus shouted. He stepped back into the corridor and snapped his fingers. That brought a pair of guards into the room, who seized the boys and dragged them out to the corridor. They were taken in two different directions. Billy tried to turn his head to see where Nik was going, but his effort was met with the back of the guard's hand against his head. Quickly, he was shoved back into the cold, dark cell he had occupied earlier. The door closed, and he was left alone and shaking.

It was hard for Billy to estimate time in such surroundings; but he was sure he had been there several hours. He had carefully made his way to a corner, and was so able to take his feet out of the water at regular intervals by propping them up against one wall while leaning against the other. The one drawback to this plan was that, for it to work, he had to sit in the water. It wasn't long before he was numb. All at once, the door opened, and a guard ordered him out. This time, he followed without hesitation. The guard escorted him down the long corridor, clutching him by the arm. Billy's progress was slow, owing to the fact that his legs were stiff from the cold water. He assumed, with some dread, that he would be put back in the hot room where Nik was earlier. Perhaps, he hoped, Nik would be waiting for him.

Then Billy thought for a moment that he had felt a slight ringing in his ears and shook his head to try to get rid of it. A moment later, he heard a single, sharp popping sound from behind him. The guard next to him twitched instinctively, so Billy assumed he heard it as well. Suddenly, the guard fell forward on his face at Billy's feet. Billy looked down and saw what looked like a small metal dart protruding from the back of the guard's neck. The confusing sight caused Billy to falter. Grabbing the wall for support, he turned to look behind him and was amazed to see Uncle Will rushing toward him. He was still holding his .45. The old man threw his arms around Billy to keep him from collapsing.

"Come on, boy. We're leaving."

"Did you...did you just kill him?!" Billy squeaked.

"No," Uncle Will responded, bending down to pull the dart from the fallen guard's neck. "But, his head will be killing him when he wakes up. Let's go!"

The rush of adrenaline gave Billy the strength to keep going. They made their way down the corridor, moving close to the wall, with Uncle Will leading the way. He stopped in front of a door and reached into his coat pocket. Pulling out a small pen-like object, he opened it to reveal a lock pick. He began to work the lock. In a moment, the door was open. Billy peered in and found Nik squatting on the floor, squinting into the light. He rushed in and grabbed his relieved friend by the arm. They exchanged no words. Their faces said it all. The three were soon making their way toward a narrow stairway that led upwards.

Once they reached the top of the stairs, Uncle Will carefully peered around the corner. Checking that their way was clear, he led them along another corridor. Suddenly, Uncle Will stopped in front of a door. It bore a small placard that read: *Oberleutnant Janus*. Uncle Will took out his lock pick and opened the door. The room was unoccupied and furnished with a heavy wooden desk and a few chairs. On the desk were a number of gray folders. The three studied the room for a moment. Uncle Will stepped toward the desk and began to rifle through the folders. Billy moved to his side and read over his shoulder. Most of what he saw made little sense to him. The papers were mostly drawings and technical diagrams, printed in German. Uncle Will, however, seemed taken aback by what he saw.

"Oh dear. This is not good."

"What is it?" asked Billy.

"He's already gone and done it."

"Done what?"

"These are plans for new super weapons that the Nazis were trying to develop, without much success. Look at this." Uncle Will handed Billy a folder. Billy and Nik studied it. The documents inside were written in English, with the United States Department of State insignia at the top of some pages. The pages were all stamped with the word 'UMBRA.' A more careful inspection showed that they were dated in February of 1998.

"What is this stuff?" Billy asked, handing it back to Uncle Will.

"These are documents pertaining to weapon designs that the U.S. was working on in the mid to late 1990's. He's apparently using these designs to perfect the Nazi weapons."

"So what does 'umbra' mean?" Nik asked.

Uncle Will replied, "That's a step above top secret. It means this stuff is highly sensitive."

"What does all this mean?"

"It means, boys, that Janus is helping the Nazis win the war. He's changing history to suit his plans." With that, Uncle Will scooped up the papers and stuffed them inside his shirt. "Marcus was supposed to have taken care of these German documents. Janus obviously took him out of the picture to keep that from happening, so I guess we'll have to."

"Where are we going?" Billy asked.

"We need to get out of here first," his uncle replied.

Uncle Will turned toward the door, but then hesitated. He looked inquisitively at a file cabinet in the corner.

"Just a second, boys. We're not leaving yet."

Billy rolled his eyes. Uncle Will opened one drawer and began thumbing through the folders. He stopped abruptly when he encountered a folder labeled: *Ravensbrouk.* He lifted it from the drawer and brought it to the desk. Billy was immediately at his side. Uncle Will picked up a pen from the desk and began to mark one of the papers, crossing out some information and jotting down some more.

"What are you doing?" Billy asked.

"Doing someone a favor," Uncle Will answered. "This is a list of people scheduled for termination at this concentration camp. I've just commuted their sentences. That ought to give Janus real fits!"

Uncle Will closed the folder, shoved it back into the drawer, and led the boys out of the office and along the corridor. Climbing a flight of stairs, they approached a large, spacious room with tall windows. The sunlight streaming into the room made it difficult for Billy or Nik to see without squinting. At the far end of the room were two large doors, obviously leading outside. As they quickly made their way across the room to escape, a loud voice from behind stopped them in their tracks.

"Where do you think you're going, Sheppard?"

They spun around to find Roland Peters standing in the doorway through which they had just passed. He was dressed, not in a Nazi uniform, but in a plain black suit. In the center of his necktie, though, was a gold tiepin in the shape of a swastika. He reached into his jacket and drew a small silver-plated pistol. As he did so, a small band of armed guards appeared behind him, each guard leveling a Schmeizer at the would-be escapees.

Peters continued, "I think the oberleutnant would be very interested to know where you're taking his prisoners."

A desperate Billy turned to look at his uncle, and was surprised to see that Uncle Will merely seemed annoyed. The old man rolled his eyes and heaved a sigh in contempt. Billy glanced downward to see that Uncle Will's hand was in his coat pocket.

"Peters," Uncle Will said, "I hope you'll pardon the pun; but I don't have time for this."

At that moment, Uncle Will drew his hand from his pocket to reveal that he was clutching a hand grenade. Before anyone could react, he pulled the pin and slid it like a hockey puck across the room. At the same time, he shoved Billy into Nik, who was standing near the door. The force of the shove caused both of them to fall into the door. It gave way and opened. They tumbled out the door onto the stone porch outside. The wide-eyed guards instinctively dove back through the opposite doorway to take cover, followed by an equally surprised Peters. Seconds later, the grenade exploded, sending a shrapnel-laden fireball through the entire room. Uncle Will had barely made it out the door. The force of the blast sent him reeling. He landed right on top of the two badly shaken boys. With a playful cackle, he rose and lifted them by their arms, then began running toward a stand of trees at the far end of the courtyard.

The explosion had raised an alarm within the compound where the three had found themselves. As sirens wailed, soldiers began to appear out of every building, all racing toward the source of the blast. The initial confusion allowed Uncle Will and the boys to disappear behind a long motorpool shed. They stopped to catch their breath. The boys were still quite sickened from their experience. Uncle Will reached once again into his pocket and removed the watch. Billy and Nik both let out a sigh of relief at the sight of the all-important timepiece.

"Let's blow this joint!" Uncle Will exclaimed, as he snapped open the cover.

Chapter Twenty

Stepping through the hole placed Billy, Nik, and Uncle Will on the edge of a rocky shoreline. The roar of pounding surf replaced the sounds of sirens and shouting. They looked out to see the waves washing over the rocks and onto the loose gravel under their feet. The air was filled with the smell of salt water. Further up the beach, there was a light coating of fresh snow that continued as far as the eye could see. It was also much colder than where they had been moments before. Billy and Nik began to shiver. As they turned around, high looming cliffs filled their field of vision. It was hard to make out more than a few features on the rockface; the sun was setting behind it, creating long shadows.

"Now, let's see," Uncle Will muttered, looking at the watch, "where did we end up? According to the watch, the year is 1939."

Nik said, "So we know when we are. We need to figure out where we are."

"Way ahead of you," replied Billy, as he tapped Nik on the arm and pointed to his uncle. Uncle Will was already tapping on the keys of his hand held computer.

"According to this," he said, "we're in southeastern Norway, about fifteen miles south of Oslo."

"Norway?" the boys said in unison.

"We'd better get you boys into some dry clothes." Uncle Will pointed toward a small, dilapidated cabin that stood a stone's throw away. When they reached it, they found it unoccupied. All it contained were a few wooden bushel baskets, an old kerosene lantern, and a heavy canvas tarpaulin that was folded on the floor. In the corner opposite the door was a small, black iron stove. Uncle Will took a small book of matches from one of his pockets and lit the lantern. He turned to the stove and opened the small door on the front. Seeing that there was already wood inside, he lit another match. Within minutes, a small fire was burning. He then closed the door to the cabin to keep out the cold North Sea wind. Some of it, however, found its way through the tiny window set into one of the walls. Finally, he lifted the tarpaulin and, ordering the boys to sit together on the floor in front of the stove, placed it over them.

"It's not the warmest blanket, but it'll keep you from freezing. You stay here. I'm going to see what I can scrounge in the way of dry clothing."

Billy remarked, "The last time you left, we ended up in a Nazi prison, being tortured."

Uncle Will hesitated at the door. Billy had every reason to say what he did, and he knew Uncle Will would have to agree. The old man bowed his head, adjusted his glasses, and turned around, lowering himself to face his shaking nephew.

"You got me there, boy. I saw them take you away on the truck. I assumed from her absence that Anastasia was not as fortunate as you were." The mention of her name compelled Nik to shut his eyes and lower his head. Billy stared. Uncle Will placed an assuring hand on his shoulder. "I couldn't just rush in there with those goons armed to the teeth. It would have cost us any chance of stopping Janus or getting home. I'm only sorry that I didn't get to you sooner. I did the best I could."

"But Anastasia's dead!" Billy snapped.

"Yes, I know," replied Uncle Will. "I'm not exactly thrilled about that either, you know! But you boys need to understand that she didn't belong to you. She belongs to history." Uncle Will rose to his full height and opened the door. "I promise I won't be long. Besides, if we didn't know where we are until a few minutes ago, Janus won't know either."

Once he was gone, the boys huddled close together, trying to keep as warm as possible until his return. They didn't speak, but they both knew each other well enough to know what the other was thinking. They were really going to miss her. Billy began to feel pangs of guilt at having been jealous about her friendship with Nik. For a moment, he thought that, in some way, she had been taken away from them for that very reason.

"Nik, I know I said this before, but I'm really sorry about all of this."

"Don't worry about it," Nik said. "I'm sure you didn't mean for this to happen."

"And I'm sorry about Anastasia," Billy continued.

"Why do you say that?" Nik turned and looked at him.

"I know you two were really…" Billy's voice trailed off. He started to feel like he was rubbing salt in an open wound. Nik cracked half a smile and shook his head.

"What?" Billy looked at him apprehensively.

Nik responded, "Actually, she talked more about you than anything else."

Billy's jaw dropped. For a moment, he forgot he was cold.

"Get out!"

"I'm serious," Nik nodded. "She was always asking me about you."

Billy sputtered, "But, you two spent so much time together, talking and stuff. And then there was that party we went to. I figured..."

"She only spent most of her time with me because I speak Russian. I must confess that I liked the attention, but it was really you she was interested in. At the party, I did not really mean to barge in on you like that. At the time I thought it was funny. I thought you would get another chance."

The boys sat silent for a moment, while Billy digested what his friend was telling him. In one way, he found it ironic that he had always assumed she would favor Nik over him. The fact that she was no longer with them made that irony sting.

"You really liked her, didn't you?" Nik asked.

"Oh, and you didn't either!" Billy retorted.

"I did," Nik replied, "but I was worried that you were getting jealous, and I didn't want her to come between us."

Billy couldn't help his nervous laughter. "I thought the same thing."

They sat silently again, listening to the pounding surf outside, folding their arms for warmth.

"When you really stop to think about it," Billy said, "it wouldn't have worked out for either of us. As hard as it is to admit, we really should have left well enough alone." Billy paused. "I'm really going to miss her."

Nik nodded, directing his eyes downward.

After what seemed like an hour, the door opened, and Uncle Will stepped in cradling a bundle in his arms. Billy and Nik jumped to their feet as he opened the bundle to reveal two thick wool sweaters and an identical pair of dark blue pea coats, similar to those worn by seamen. They tore voraciously at the garments, donning them with as much speed as their numb, shaking hands would allow.

"I'm sorry this is all I could come up with," said Uncle Will. His remark went unheeded, as they boys were clearly relieved to have what was there. They returned to their places in front of the stove, rubbing their hands together, happy to be rid of their soggy shirts. Uncle Will sat down next to them and took his orbital displacement calculator from his coat pocket. He tapped a few keys and studied the screen intently.

"What's up?" asked Billy.

Uncle Will replied absently, "I'm trying to figure out how to get us home."

"Home in Cannon Falls?"

"No. Home in England."

Uncle Will tapped a few more keys and waited. The machine beeped an answer to him, to which he responded in disgust.

"According to this," he explained, "if we go back to 1889 from here, we'll end up in the middle of the Sahara Desert. We'll also miss Cannon Falls by several decades."

"So, what are we going to do?" Nik asked through chattering teeth.

"Well," Uncle Will continued, "the quickest, easiest way to get back to England in 1889 is to leave 1939 from here." With that, he held the computer up in front of the boys to show them the screen. On it was a map of Europe. A red spot indicated the location from which they would be able to get back. It was located in the middle of the North Sea.

"That's just great!" Billy spat in frustration. "How the heck are we supposed to..."

He was interrupted by Uncle Will gesturing for silence and looking apprehensively at the door. As the room fell silent, the sounds of voices could be heard in the distance. Uncle Will grabbed the lantern and blew out the flame. In the darkness, the three could see the light of a distant lantern shining through the window. They huddled in the corner and waited. Billy was horrified as he imagined being captured by Janus again. The lights drew closer, until they were visible through the cracks around the flimsy door. Uncle Will placed his hand inside his coat, ready to draw his gun. At once the door crashed in, and the room was filled with blinding light. When their eyes adjusted, Uncle Will and the boys could see that they were clearly outgunned.

Three men stood in the doorway, the one in the center holding a large searchlight. He was a very large man with blond hair and a thick blond beard, wearing a long, heavy black coat. The other two leveled rifles at the three people sitting on the floor. They were similarly dressed. The man with the light spoke.

"Gentlemen," he said in a noticeable Norwegian accent, "please stand up and place your hands in the air."

They did as they were told. One of the men with the rifles slung his weapon over his shoulder and immediately began patting down each of them. Finding nothing on the boys, he moved to Uncle Will, who placed his hands in front of him and slowly opened his coat. The three captors watched intently as he slowly and deliberately lifted his pistol from its holster. He carefully presented it to them. The one who was searching him took it and handed it to the bearded one. He took it and nodded back toward Uncle Will. The other man continued to pat him down. He reached into Uncle Will's hip pocket and pulled out a wallet and the watch, handing them over as well. Billy's heart raced as he saw the watch change hands. He only hoped they would not find the computer. The man with the beard snapped the watch open and admired it. Much to the surprise of Billy and Nik, the inside of the lid bore a small photograph of Aunt Catherine, not the jeweled surface they were accustomed to seeing.

"You may have my gun," Uncle Will spoke up, "but please let me have my watch back. It is a gift from my wife. It's very dear to me."

"Fair enough," the man replied, tossing the watch through the air toward Uncle Will. He caught it effortlessly, much to the boys' relief.

"Gentlemen," the bearded man continued, "you will tell me who you are and what you are doing here."

"Everything you need to know is in there," Uncle Will responded, pointing to the wallet.

The man opened the wallet and looked inside. There, he found a few slips of paper and a card with Uncle Will's photo on it. Billy tried discretely to see what they were, but the man was standing too far away from him. The man showed the papers to the other man, who was still holding a rifle on them. They exchanged words in Norwegian.

"Mr. Sheppard," he said, "you and your companions will come with us."

With that, he turned and exited the cabin, gesturing for Uncle Will and boys to follow. As they reluctantly went along, the two riflemen exited and closed the door. The group walked along the shoreline for several hundred yards, until they came to a small truck. One rifleman climbed into the driver's seat, and the rest climbed into the back. Soon, they were underway, moving up the hill toward a village in the distance.

"Where are we going?" Billy ventured.

The bearded one responded, "Where we are going is no concern of yours."

"Well," Uncle Will said, "at least you can tell us who you might be. After all, I've told you who I am."

"It is hardly important; but if it matters so much to you, you may call me Bjorn."

The truck continued its bumpy trek up the hill, its transmission grinding in protest.

"Bjorn," Uncle Will continued, "how did you know to speak English to us back there?"

"We didn't. We only heard a few English words as we approached."

"Then wouldn't it be safe to say that we're Americans?"

"No, it wouldn't." Bjorn's answer surprised them. "How do I know English is your first language?"

"Ah," Uncle Will laughed. "Let's say, for instance, that we were German spies." This brought a stern glance from Bjorn. "Even if we spoke English as well as any Englishman, would we speak it to each other when we assumed we were alone and unobserved?"

Bjorn thought for a moment, but was still generally unconvinced. He simply folded his arms and studied Uncle Will's face.

Eventually, the truck had reached much smoother conditions, and lumbered down a narrow street through the center of the village. The passengers in the back felt it turn a sharp corner and then stop. The driver got out and opened the back doors, ordering Uncle Will and the boys out at gunpoint. They were led into a small cottage that was situated within a thick stand of snow covered spruce trees. A dim orange glow emanated from the windows, as white smoke curled from the chimney. To Billy, the whole scene looked like some caricature of a Christmas card. The entire group made its way into the cottage.

In the front sitting room, a few heavy chairs sat in no particular order. A fire blazed in the fireplace, providing the only light in the room. Directly in front of the fire, a large chair with a high back was situated. The only part of the chair's occupant that was visible was a thin hand resting on the arm. Uncle Will and the boys were directed to wait by the door, along with the two riflemen. Bjorn approached the chair and leaned toward it, holding out Uncle Will's wallet and papers. The seemingly disembodied hand reached out and took them. After a moment, a small scratchy voice spoke from the chair in very low tones. Bjorn stood upright, nodded, and turned to the captives.

"Wait here. Do not move." With that, he turned on his heels and stepped through a doorway on the opposite end of the room. As their eyes followed him, Billy and Nik hardly noticed when the person in the chair rose and faced them. When they did, all they could see was a frail silhouette against the firelight. The figure slowly moved toward them. Again the scratchy voice spoke.

"Jan, please turn on the lights." The accent was unmistakably German, making Billy and Nik cringe. "Do not make our guests stand in the dark."

The rifleman to their left immediately reached over to a switch on the wall and filled the room with light from the small chandelier hanging overhead. Billy and Nik nearly gasped at the sight before them. Their host was a thin, gaunt figure with almost skeleton-like features. His silver hair was combed back firmly against his scalp. His eyes were difficult to gauge, hiding behind thick, dark, almost black, glasses. Down the right side of his face was an angry white scar. It ran in a straight vertical line from his hairline to his chin, interrupted only by his right eye. He wore a long red velvet robe with a sash. It reached to his knees, revealing only the bottoms of his dark trousers. Smiling at his guests, he gestured to them with a withered hand.

"Please, come and warm yourselves by the fire." They slowly, reluctantly did so. "I trust that these men have treated you well."

"Quite," Uncle Will replied. "Would you mind telling us who you are?"

The old man chuckled, "That, mein fruend, very much depends on who you are." As he spoke, Bjorn reappeared with Uncle Will's papers. "Ah, Bjorn. What have you found?"

Bjorn handed the man a sheet of paper and returned the wallet and other items to Uncle Will. For the first time since they had met him at the cabin, Bjorn smiled to his prisoners. He spoke sharply in Norwegian to the man who had searched them. The man quickly reached into his pocket and drew out Uncle Will's gun. In the same motion, he handed it back to him. Uncle Will quickly holstered it under his jacket.

"Herr Sheppard," the old man said, "I am pleased, and relieved, to meet you. I am Dr. Irwin Fremdelieb." He turned and addressed his men. "These men are our guests. See that they are comfortable."

The men immediately placed their rifles against the wall and moved three of the chairs closer to the fire. Dr. Fremdelieb invited them to sit. After a few minutes, the three of them were sipping hot coffee.

"Dr. Fremdelieb," Uncle Will said, "you still haven't told me who you are."

"My apologies, Herr Sheppard. We have to be very careful to whom we reveal such things. I am a scientist, a physicist to be precise. I escaped from Germany some months ago. You see, in addition to being a scientist, I am also - how do you say - a pacifist. That is not an easy thing to be in Germany right now. At least, they did not make it very easy for me." He pointed to his scar with a shaky finger. "I managed to escape with the help of certain British agents."

"So why here?" Billy asked hesitantly. "Why Norway? Why would the British bring you to Norway?"

"Because, young man," Fremdelieb continued, "I have chosen to come here."

"Chosen?"

"It was only last year that scientists in Germany discovered atomic fission. They are not far from developing a new weapon that uses this process to create a destructive force the power of which we can only imagine. In the hands of the Nazis, this weapon will mean..." His already shaking voice trailed off, as he clenched his fist to regain his composure. "I dare not think of it!"

"I think I know where you're going with this," Uncle Will continued for him. "In order to create such a weapon the Nazis need a substance called deuterium oxide, also known as 'heavy water.' The only place in the world that can produce large quantities of it is not very far from here."

Dr. Fremdelieb nodded, "Norsk Hydro, in Ryukan. I am here to keep tabs on the plant's output for British Intelligence. They are close, very close."

"Perhaps I can be of some help," Uncle Will responded, reaching inside the back of his coat. "I have something that could help you and your British friends. All I ask in return is a flight out of here."

Uncle Will produced one of the thick file folders he had taken from Janus' office at the Nazi compound. He handed it to Dr. Fremdelieb. As the old scientist pored over the documents, his eyebrows slowly crept upward. His hands shook even more.

"Where did you find this?!"

"I'm afraid I can't say," answered Uncle Will. Billy and Nik looked at each other, both trying to stifle their excitement.

"I must get this to the British immediately!" Dr. Fremdelieb shouted. "But how?" He paused to think. "I know! The British Naval Attaché has an office in Oslo. I shall bring it there. You need not worry, Herr Sheppard. I will not reveal its source."

"Can you get us out of here?" Uncle Will asked.

"Yes, I can," the old man beamed. "Bjorn!" The door opened and in stepped the big Norwegian. "Notify Edvard. These men need a flight to Britain immediately!"

Several hours later, Billy and Nik stood yawning at each other, stamping their feet against the cold, on the rocky shore they had occupied the previous afternoon. Uncle Will stood with Bjorn, looking out intently over the water. It would be dawn within an hour. The small cabin where they were found stood several yards away. Inside the cabin, Jan, with his trusty rifle slung behind his shoulder, was busy at a large radio set. The thin wire aerial was strung out the window and festooned across the edge of the roof. He listened intently to his headset, turning the large black dials on his receiver. After a moment, he took off his headset and stepped outside.

He called to Bjorn in near perfect English, "They're on their way, sir. I'll ready the beacon."

He returned to the cabin, and then emerged again with what appeared to be a large lantern with a highly polished reflector attached to one side. Striking a match, he lit it, spraying a narrow beam of bright light out over the pounding sea. Billy, Nik, and Uncle Will strained to see what was out over the water. Within a minute, they could see a dark shape moving parallel to the shoreline, drawing closer and closer to the water. Eventually, it landed; and a minute later, a small rubber raft was visible, bobbing on the waves. When it approached the shore, a man in a uniform of the R.A.F. stepped onto the sand. He was a short, stocky fellow with dark hair and dark eyes.

"Lieutenant Quinnlan at your service," he half shouted. "Who are my passengers?"

"These three," Bjorn replied, motioning to Uncle Will and the boys.

"Right! Let's be off then."

Uncle Will stepped forward. "You received my instructions? I called for three parachutes to be provided."

"We have them," answered the lieutenant, "but I doubt very much that you'll need them. This aircraft is quite safe."

"Let's be off then."

A short while later, Uncle Will, Billy, Nik and the lieutenant were aboard the huge gray seaplane, a Short Sunderland Flying Boat. Her four engines were only idling, but still managed to kick up enough water to thoroughly spray down the raft's occupants. A small ladder extended from a hatch just behind the wing. Under the wing was another large opening from which protruded a machine gun. Once inside, Uncle Will and the boys settled up against a bulkhead. Lieutenant Quinnlan stepped past them and made his way to the cockpit. Seconds later, the engines roared to full throttle and the heavy plane bounced along the waves until she lifted off.

As the sunlight began to appear behind them, Uncle Will scanned the interior of the airplane, looking for the promised parachutes. He found them stowed in the rear compartment. Steadying himself against the bulkheads, he made his way toward the cockpit. Billy and Nik, unable to catch up on any sleep due to the roaring of the engines, opted to follow him. In the cockpit, Lieutenant Quinnlan sat in the copilot's position. The pilot, an older, red-haired individual with bulbous eyes held the control yoke firmly. When Quinnlan noticed Uncle Will, he tapped the pilot on the shoulder.

"Captain MacAfee," he shouted, "this is Mr. Sheppard."

MacAfee extended a hand to Uncle Will to shake his, as Quinnlan took the controls.

"A pleasure to have you aboard sir." His accent was a thick Scottish.

Uncle Will reached into his pocket and took out a slip of paper. He handed it to the captain.

"I need you to fly to these coordinates. Please notify me immediately when we get there."

"Will do, Mr. Sheppard." MacAfee then spoke into the intercom to relay the instructions to the craft's navigator.

The boys walked back to the rear of the airplane. Finding a porthole, they looked out over the water as it sparkled in the morning sun. Uncle Will joined them.

"We'll be in the clear before long," he assured them.

A half-hour later, Quinnlan approached them, waving to Uncle Will that they had reached the coordinates. Uncle Will and the boys moved toward the cockpit. The captain sat waiting for further instructions.

"I want you to circle here, captain," Uncle Will explained. "Do not move from this position. We'll put on our parachutes."

"What?!" The captain's eyes widened. Even Quinnlan was visibly shocked. "You cannot bail out here, sir! We're still over the bloody ocean! Do you have any idea how cold that water is?!" Billy began to squirm at the mention of cold water. Nik glanced at him with an expression of dread. Uncle Will was unfazed.

"You have your instructions, captain. I've no time to argue with you."

"I'll not do it, I tell you!" the pilot protested.

Uncle Will glared at him, reached into his coat, and drew his gun. Billy and Nik abruptly stepped back. Before anyone else could react, he positioned himself behind the pilot's seat and placed the gun's muzzle firmly against the back of MacAfee's head. He stared coldly at

Lieutenant Quinnlan, who sat in the copilot's chair, gaping in horror. Uncle Will reached back into his coat with his free hand and removed his wallet. He flipped it open and showed it to Quinnlan. Inside was the card with his picture on it.

"Do you see that, Lieutenant? U.S. Department of War! I'm quite serious about this. If my instructions are not followed to the letter, there won't even be a court martial. Now, do as you're told!"

Quinnlan stared open-mouthed at the identification card, then at Uncle Will. MacAfee sat frozen in his seat. Even the boys were surprised by what was happening. The old man's really lost it now, Billy thought. Finally, Quinnlan relented.

"Yes, sir. What ever you say, sir. We'll hold our position."

"You're mad, sir," MacAfee shouted, glaring at Uncle Will.

"Yes, quite." Uncle Will simply smiled and turned to the rear of the plane. The boys followed him closely, wondering what was going through his head. He picked up a parachute and strapped it on, instructing the boys to do the same. He then walked toward the hatch they had used to board the aircraft. Lieutenant Quinnlan intercepted him.

"Sir, I must ask you to reconsider this course of action. You'll freeze to death in mere minutes down there."

"Lieutenant, you need not worry about that," Uncle Will said with cold deliberation. "You only need to do what you are asked to do. Please understand that this mission does not exist, and we were never here. Do you understand me?"

The lieutenant could see that Uncle Will was quite serious. He finally stepped aside as the door swung open. As the blast of air washed through the opening, Uncle Will motioned for the boys to step out. Billy stood there, looking out at the vast expanse of ocean below them. He thought that Uncle Will had certainly gone insane to try something like this. Then, it occurred to him that maybe he was a little crazy for being so willing to go along with it. As hard as it was to believe, they were about to leap out of a perfectly sound aircraft into a freezing ocean. He and Nik glanced at one another. At first, they hesitated; but Uncle Will discretely pulled the watch out of his pocket and showed it to them, giving a reassuring nod. With that, and a bit of coaching from Uncle Will, they were out. He turned, saluted the lieutenant, and jumped out behind them. Quinnlan stood still for a moment, shaking against the cold. The intercom crackled in his ear.

"Did they actually jump?" MacAfee's voice said. "Can you see them?"

Quinnlan dashed to the open hatch and leaned out.

"They're gone! I don't see their parachutes! I don't see anything!"

Chapter Twenty-One

Gwyneth was strolling slowly across the open, green lawn of her parents' estate. Her expression was pensive, as she gently held a white rose from the garden in her hands, inhaling its scent. Her pale blue dress fluttered in the light breeze. Across the lawn, her mother sat at the edge of the garden, working on her cross-stitch, and taking advantage of the clear weather to get some sun. Suddenly, the cloudless sky far above them was disrupted by a large black void that hovered motionless. Its appearance went unnoticed by both of them. Within seconds, it spat out three large parachutes that began to slowly descend to earth. As the shadow of one of them passed over the spot where Aunt Catherine was sitting, she looked skyward with a start.

"What on earth?!" she sputtered, leaping to her feet and dropping her cross-stitch on the grass. By now the parachutes had drifted closer to the ground.

"Hi honey! I'm home!" Uncle Will shouted to her from the air.

"William!" replied Aunt Catherine. "What are you trying to do? Get yourself killed?! And I suppose you intend to take those two dear boys with you!" She gathered her long skirts up and began to run to the spot where the chutes were landing. A very excited Gwyneth, who by now had crossed the entire width of the lawn, met her. Uncle Will was the first to land. He braced for landing and came to earth, his parachute deflating as he ran out from under it. Billy and Nik landed almost simultaneously; both tumbling head over heals in a tangled heap of rope and canvas. As they wrestled their way out of the harnesses, Billy stood face to face with his cousin, her face shining with a wide smile. As Nik tossed away the last of the thin cords of his parachute, he waved a greeting to her. As Uncle Will and Aunt Catherine approached, arm in arm, Gwyneth began to look around. All at once, the bright smile faded from her face, replaced by a look of dread.

"Where is Anastasia?" she asked.

The boys hung their heads. She spun around to face her father. He cleared his throat and directed his eyes toward the horizon. Aunt Catherine studied his face with great consternation. Gwyneth looked back at Billy, who was looking at her sorrowfully.

"What happened to Anastasia?" she demanded, her eyes welling with tears.

Billy whispered, "She didn't make it." His voice cracked as he spoke.

Gwyneth sobbed, covering her face with her hands. Billy rushed to her and threw his arms around her, and she pressed her tear soaked face into his shoulder. It was an immense struggle for Billy not to start crying himself. Nik stepped forward and placed a hand on her arm.

"What happened?" asked Aunt Catherine. She too was fighting to maintain her composure.

Uncle Will answered, "Janus got hold of her. There was nothing we could do." After a few moments of silence, Uncle Will spoke again. "We need to get these two into some clean clothes." The whole group made their way toward the house. Billy kept his arm around Gwyneth as they slowly walked.

After much needed, and even more appreciated, hot baths and changes of clothes, Billy and Nik emerged from the house to find the others in the garden. Gwyneth sat on the hard stone bench, her hands in her lap, twisting a wet handkerchief around her fingers. Her parents strolled among the rose bushes. Occasionally, they would stop, and Aunt Catherine would rest her head on Uncle Will's shoulder. The boys entered the garden and immediately headed for the stone bench. They placed themselves on either side of Gwyneth, as she dabbed her eyes with the handkerchief. Carefully, they related to her the full story of what had happened to Anastasia in the watch shop.

"I just can't believe she's gone," she whispered. The boys simply nodded in response. "We were getting along so well. She seemed so happy here. I don't know if she ever told you; but she was so very grateful to both of you for saving her. She really admired you both. She told me so." Again, Gwyneth started to cry. The boys looked at each other over her bowed head, wondering what to do next. They easily concluded that there was nothing to be done.

The afternoon sun was dipping behind the house, casting a large shadow across the view from the library. Billy was walking along the upper gallery, absently browsing through the thousands of books that lined the shelves. Many of them were glanced over without any notice. Billy was simply trying to give his mind something to do besides thinking of Anastasia. For a moment he was taken by the sheer size of his uncle's collection of books. There seemed to be a book on every conceivable subject. Most were history books, which seemed natural, especially when Billy recalled their visit to Marcus Straker in the insane asylum.

As he slowly drifted past row after row of books, something caught his eye. He stopped and looked carefully at one of the books in front of him. It was a large thick book entitled "The History of Tsarist Russia." He carefully slid the book off the shelf and began to leaf through it, not even really looking at what it had to say. He stopped immediately when he came to a section of illustrations and photographs in the middle of the book. There on the page was a picture of Tsar Nicolas II and his family, including Anastasia. She was much younger in this picture, taken years before the Revolution. Billy felt a lump in his throat. He turned around and leaned against the bookshelf, flipping the page.

The next page carried individual portraits of the family. Almost in the middle of the page was a portrait of Anastasia, dressed in royal attire, with a crown on her head. Her eyes were looking away with a serious expression. It almost looked as if posing for this picture was the last thing she wanted to do. Billy stood motionless, staring at the picture, wishing desperately to make it real, and hardly noticing that he was sliding down the bookcase. He sat there on the floor of the gallery, never taking his eyes off of hers for a second. As he cradled the book in his lap, he touched the face in the picture, a face that didn't bear the scar to which he had become accustomed. He tried but failed to keep from shaking. Before he was aware enough to stop them, tears were running down his cheeks.

Billy never even realized that Uncle Will had appeared next to him. Uncle Will looked down at the pictures on the page, sighed, patted his nephew on the shoulder, and walked down the stairs to the ground level. Gwyneth had observed the whole situation from an adjacent room and quietly rushed to meet her father at the base of the stairs. She was visibly upset.

"Father..."

Uncle Will put his hand toward her to stop her from going upstairs. "Just leave him alone for now," he whispered.

Gwyneth looked up at her sobbing cousin, and then shifted her gaze to the floor. After some hesitation she spoke.

"Did he really have such feelings for her?"

Uncle Will thought for a moment and answered, "I guess it would have been hard not to."

Later that evening, the reunited family sat in the library. No one spoke. Aunt Catherine did not work on her cross-stitch, nor did Gwyneth play and sing at the piano. The only sound was that of the giant grandfather clock at the far end of the room, ticking monotonously. Uncle Will sat at his desk, poring over the remainder of the files he had taken from Janus' office at the Nazi compound in Holland. What remained were the U.S. State Department papers. As he studied them, his eyes grew wider and wider.

"Oh, ho," he laughed, "this is heavy stuff!" Everyone else in the room glanced toward him, startled at the sudden breach of silence.

Billy rose from his place on the sofa and approached the desk. Uncle Will handed him a few of the papers.

"It's fairly common knowledge that the Germans were very close to developing an atomic bomb when they lost the war," he explained. "Janus was apparently going to make sure they succeeded, and then some. These are the plans for a small scale, tactical nuclear warhead. The pencil drawings on that last page are Janus'. He came up with a way to adapt that warhead to the German V2 rocket." Billy nodded absently as he continued to study the papers, and Uncle Will continued to explain their contents. "These other documents show the location and inventory of chemical weapons in the Middle East in the late twentieth century, as well as other nuclear weapons. Janus was obviously going to make sure he had all bases covered."

"Chemical weapons?" asked Billy.

"Yes, wonderful little cocktails like anthrax, botulin, VX. The sorts of things that could really ruin someone's day if they don't give Janus what he wants."

"Father," Gwyneth interrupted, "what are these things you're talking about?"

Uncle Will looked at her over the top of his glasses. "They're things that we're going to wish we could un-invent. But you don't need to concern yourself with them."

Billy listened carefully to what his uncle said to her. It began to make sense to him why Uncle Will chose to keep his family in a completely different time period, why he kept Gwyneth here in the 1880's, and not in what was to him the present time. She indeed would not have to worry about such things. To be sure, there would be problems to deal with, but not like these. He thought of how fortunate she was that her father had the power to protect her this way. At the same time, he couldn't help wondering if Uncle Will wasn't being a bit unrealistic. Uncle Will interrupted his train of thought.

"I have a very good idea where he got most of this information, so I think it's accurate; but I don't know for sure." He stood up and began to pace in front of the fireplace, still studying the files.

"What do you mean, Mr. Sheppard?" asked Nik.

Without looking up, Uncle Will answered, "I used to have a few connections at the State Department."

"Connections?" Billy asked suspiciously, recalling the identification card his uncle showed the crew of the flying boat.

"Yeah, connections," came the abrupt reply.

Uncle Will continued to pace for a while, engrossed in deep thought about the papers he held.

"Billy, I need you and Nik to return to my workshop," he announced.

"Why can't you come with us?" Billy protested. He had no trouble reminding himself of what happened the last time he took the watch and traveled without his uncle. He also remembered how displeased Uncle Will was with the results. Even worse was the still fresh memory of Anastasia.

"I need to take care of a few things here," Uncle Will replied. He could see Billy's apprehension. "Don't worry. You'll be fine. If you leave at sunrise tomorrow, the watch should put you at the southeast corner of John Katter's field in Cannon Falls. Go to the workshop and look in the old filing cabinet. There's a folder labeled 'State Department.' Bring it back here. Just make sure you return from the same place you arrive."

"But..."

"But nothing. We need to find out how accurate this information is," Uncle Will insisted. "It's settled. You two will leave tomorrow."

The following dawn, while the sun was still behind the trees, two bleary-eyed boys sat on the patio behind the house. Billy and Nik stared blankly into space, waiting for Uncle Will. They had already changed into T-shirts and jeans. When the glass doors to the patio opened, it was not Uncle Will, but Gwyneth who greeted them. She was wearing a simple gray dress. Her hair, which was usually up in a tight bun, was hanging down around her shoulders. Billy looked at her and forced a smile. As she approached, he noticed something else that looked different about her, as if something were missing. He was too tired, and too anxious, to put his finger on it.

"I just wanted to see you off," she whispered. The boys wearily stood up, and she kissed each of them gently on the cheek. "I hope I see you again, very soon." With that, she turned and walked back into the house, pausing at the door to look back at them. As she turned again to enter the house, Aunt Catherine met her in the doorway. After kissing her on the forehead, she walked out onto the patio. Aunt Catherine gestured for Billy to approach. He looked up at Aunt Catherine and saw that tears were starting to appear in her eyes.

"I'll be praying for you," she whispered. "You don't need to be afraid. The Creator of time itself is with you."

She held his hands in hers for a moment, and then turned to go back into the house.

Finally, Uncle Will appeared, his eyes following his wife across the patio. Removing the watch from his pocket, he wound it, set the time, and held it out to Billy.

"Uncle Will, I don't get it," Billy said nervously. "Why are they acting like we might not see each other again? Why aren't you coming with us?"

"I need to stay here in case Janus gets ahead of us. Your aunt and cousin are very aware of that possibility," Uncle Will explained.

"I don't..."

"Billy, you'll do just fine," his uncle assured him. "I know what you're thinking; and I want you to know that I never stopped trusting you with this. When I gave it to you, it was for keeps. Once Janus is stopped, that's it. The Guild is finished."

Billy took the watch from his uncle. His eyes widened with excitement as the morning sun reflected from its gold case. He looked at his uncle, then back at the watch, then again at his uncle. Suddenly, he stepped forward and threw his arms around Uncle Will's stout middle, giving him a vigorous bearhug.

"I won't let you down, Uncle Will."

Billy turned to face Nik, and the two nodded purposefully. Billy opened the cover of the watch and pointed it toward the rising sun.

Chapter Twenty-Two

Billy and Nik emerged at the location Uncle Will mentioned. It was about the same time of day that they had left Cannon Falls. Billy knew from experience that it would take them at least fifteen minutes to reach his house, if they ran. They did just that, and arrived at the back of Billy's yard just in time to see Billy's father, Steve, pull his van into the driveway, having returned from work. The boys ducked behind the garage, peering out to see if Steve observed them. He got out of the van and walked with a tired gait into the house. They hadn't been seen.

Billy whispered, "We can't go in through the house. They think we're still in the basement." Nik nodded. Billy then pointed to a small window set into the foundation of the house, located directly across the yard from their position. Nik nodded again. He knew what Billy had in mind.

Billy had used that very window many times to gain entry when he forgot to carry his house key and no one was home to let him in. Quickly, they sidled across the lawn to the window. Billy tried it and was relieved to find that it was still unlocked. Swinging it up and inside, he stretched his torso through the narrow opening and hooked the sash onto a small eyebolt that was set into one of the rafters in the basement. Within seconds, the boys were inside. When they reached the workshop door, Billy took the watch from his pocket. At the other end of the chain was the key Uncle Will had given him. They entered the workshop and locked the door behind them.

At once, they got to work. Billy went to the old file cabinet next to the workbench and began to look for the requested file. Many of the folders inside were tattered and filled with brittle, yellow paper. Toward the back was a file that looked much newer. It bore the words 'State Department.' Pay dirt. Billy pulled the file from the drawer. Inside was a white sheet of paper with some handwriting on it. It read:

William:
I told you he could get inside!
Marcus

As Billy continued to thumb through the file, he found a photograph. Its blurred image looked like a print made from a video signal. It showed a narrow corridor with a man in a brown tweed jacket walking away from the camera. He held a briefcase in his hand. Although the man was of roughly the same build as Janus, he had a full head of hair. Obviously a hairpiece, Billy thought. The remaining item in the folder was a photocopy of a magazine article. Billy quickly skimmed over it. It told of a man in a brown tweed jacket walking into the executive office of the Secretary of State and leaving with a number of sensitive documents. Billy turned to see Nik studying the wire recorder, which was still on the bench. His attention was drawn to it, because Nik seemed to have found something.

"What's up?"

"Look here on the supply spool." It was still on the machine; its load of wire already passed to the take-up reel. At first, Billy noticed nothing new. Then Nik pointed under the top flange of the reel. Tucked under it were several more turns of wire. Both boys stared at it in amazement.

Billy said, "The wire must have snapped. We didn't hear the whole thing!"

Nik was already threading the wire onto the machine. He threw the switch to start it running. They listened as the voice of Marcus Straker continued where he had left off. Although the words sounded erratic and disjointed, they began to make sense.

"William, he's found out about them. You've got to get them out of England before it's too late. He has the file. He's coming for me. I've heard rumors about what he's done to the others. If that's what's waiting for me, I hope I can..."

At that point, the wire ran out. That was the end of it.

"Now what are we going to do?" asked Billy.

"Maybe we have all the information we need," Nik said. "We need to tell your uncle that his family is in danger. He will know what to do."

Billy could see that his friend was right. "Yeah, let's get going. We need to hurry." He pointed to the window to indicate that the sun was beginning to set. They immediately slipped out of the same window they had entered and then out of the yard. After another short run, they found themselves at the edge of John Katter's field, where it bordered the road. Finding the same dirt path they followed out of the field, they headed southeast. As they walked, Billy took the watch from his pocket. He handed the file folder to Nik, so his hands would be free to set the time. The southeast corner of the field was situated in a large natural depression in the land. This was ideal, as it would help to conceal their departure, as it had their arrival. They stood at the edge of a row of thick corn, and Billy opened the watch.

The watch placed them at the edge of the woods adjoining Uncle Will's estate in England. The air was clear and quiet as they made their way to the back of the house. There was no sign of Uncle Will or the others. Billy assumed aloud that they were still waiting inside. The two dogs came from around the side of the house and ambled toward the boys. Billy put his hand out for the first dog to sniff. The dogs had grown accustomed to Billy and Nik in the time they had spent there. After the brief encounter, the dogs made their way to a small outbuilding that served as a combination tool shed, barn, and home for the dogs. Billy and Nik continued toward the house, growing more unsettled by the stillness.

They reached the patio and the high wrought iron and glass wall that made up the south end of the house. There was a narrow door set into the glass and iron work that lead directly into the library. As they entered the house, Billy fully expected to be met by his uncle. The room was deserted.

"Uncle Will?" he called. His eyes scanned the library. There was no answer. He dropped the folder they had retrieved from the workshop on Uncle Will's desk.

"Something's not right," he said. Nik glanced at him as if he were stating the obvious.

The two immediately split up and began walking through the entire house, calling for Uncle Will, Aunt Catherine and Gwyneth. No response. They returned to the library. They did find the clothes they had left behind, so they changed into them.

"They would not have left without telling you," Nik said, sounding as if he were trying to convince himself as much as Billy.

"You don't suppose Janus got here before we did?" Billy responded, nearly choking on the words. He started to feel a knot in his stomach. He looked at Nik and noticed that he was squinting. His face shone from a bright light being directed toward him. Billy moved toward him to see where it was coming from. Nik was already pointing out the source.

"The sunlight is reflecting off that globe."

The polished brass of the map of England on the globe was shining brightly, with both pointers on the large rings surrounding it aimed almost one on top of the other. One pointer was placed on a gold star set at the location of Leeds, right where the boys were. The other was positioned close by in London. Billy looked up at the concentric rings over the latter and read the date.

"September 15, 1939."

When he compared the date on the Leeds pointer to the date on the watch, the two were the same. Then something occurred to Billy.

"This thing's been moved."

Nik asked, "What makes you say that."

"Because the last time I saw it, these pointers were not this close together. Besides, it wasn't reflecting sunlight in that direction when we left, and that was only a few minutes ago."

"So what are you getting at?"

"I'm wondering if, somehow, they went there." Billy pointed to London on the globe.

"And you think we should go there to look for them." Nik did not sound enthusiastic about that idea.

"Well, what else should we do?"

Nik drew a deep breath. "I think we should wait here." He was interrupted by Billy rolling his eyes, but he continued. "At least for a little while."

Billy paused and considered Nik's words. Waiting a short while wouldn't make that much difference. He agreed. They sat and waited for about a half an hour.

Billy found it hard to sit still. He began browsing the library, occasionally taking a book from the shelf, flipping idly through it, and replacing it. At one point, he came to the spiral staircase that led to the top tier of the room. He looked up and recognized the book that contained the picture of Anastasia. He took a few steps up the stairs, and then paused. No, he thought. It would only hurt. He needed to let her go. The chiming of the clock interrupted his thoughts.

That was all the waiting Billy could stand. He descended the stairs.

"Let's go. Something is definitely not right here."

Nik was compelled to agree, and so Billy set the watch and off they went.

Chapter Twenty-Three

They hadn't even considered where the watch would take them. The globe was nowhere near as accurate as the computer, which was missing along with Uncle Will. Had they taken this into account, they perhaps would not have been as surprised that they had ended up in a hospital room; nor would they have been as ill prepared for what unfolded. The room was clean, but drab, decorated in very subdued tones. The lights were out, and the only light in the room seeped in through the edges of the drawn curtains.

As Billy's eyes adjusted, he scanned the room and saw a man asleep on the bed. The man slept on top of the covers, wearing pajamas and a robe. Billy and Nik stood at the foot of the bed, not sure of what to do next. They traded uneasy glances, afraid to speak even in a whisper. Billy snapped the cover of the watch shut. The man stirred and awoke. Since the man was on his side, he didn't spot his two visitors right away. They froze. The man seemed to sense he was being watched, because he suddenly turned and sat up, his eyes wide with terror.

The shriek he made caused them both to literally jump.

"Who are you?! What do you want?! Help!!"

Billy put his hands up in a gesture of assurance that went ignored. Nik simply hung his head and sighed.

"Sir," Billy began, "it's okay. We're not going to hurt you. We just took a wrong turn somewhere."

"Janus sent you, didn't he?" was the response.

"Sir, I'm sorry. We just came into the wrong..." Billy caught himself. "What did you say?"

"I don't know anything about any watch." As the man said this he placed his arm across the pillow, as if something underneath it were about to leap out. His eyes shifted nervously.

"What watch?" Nik asked.

"I don't know anything!"

Billy stepped forward. "Has Janus been here?"

"Don't touch me!" The man leaped to his feet and stood in the middle of the bed.

Billy backed away. This is getting nowhere, he thought.

"We were not sent by Dr. Janus," Billy explained in slow careful tones. "My uncle is William Shepperd. Do you know him?"

The man became visibly less hysterical, but stood his ground.

"What if I do?" he asked suspiciously.

"We're trying to find him. He may be in trouble, and if he is, Janus is behind it."

Billy could see that the man still wasn't convinced. He looked down at his hip pocket, where he had put the watch. Thrusting his hand in, he looked at Nik for assurance. Nik nodded. Billy took out the watch and held it out to the man.

"This is my uncle's watch. Have you seen it before?"

When the man's eyes fell on the watch, they immediately welled up with tears. He stepped carefully off the bed and reached out for the watch. Billy reluctantly released it as the man cradled it tenderly. Although the man's mouth was wide open, no sound came for a moment. When it did come, it was half sobbing, half laughter.

"It's true!" he said, "They're still out there!"

He held the watch to his ear and closed his eyes as he listened to its hypnotic ticking. For a moment, it seemed like he was completely unaware of his surroundings.

Just then, the door burst open, and there appeared a nurse. She was a small, thin, young woman with reddish hair, neatly tucked beneath her cap. Her eyes were wide with shock as she spotted the two boys.

"What on Earth?!" Here we go again, Billy thought.

The man snapped back to reality with a jolt. Glancing at the nurse, he quickly wiped the tears from his cheek with the sleeve of his robe. She rushed toward him.

"Rupert," she said in a scolding tone, "what is going on here?"

Before he could answer, she wheeled around and confronted the two boys, placing herself between them and Rupert as if she were protecting him from attack.

"Who are you? How did you get in here?"

Again, before Billy or Nik could respond, she was helping Rupert back into bed. He raised not the slightest protest. When she saw the watch in his hand, she looked even more agitated.

"Where did you get that, Rupert?"

"Grace," he spoke in a reassuring tone, "it's all right. It belongs to that young man there." He pointed to Billy.

She turned and said to Billy, "You may have it back now." It sounded like an order.

Billy took the watch from Rupert and observed as Nurse Grace stepped closer to Rupert, placing her arm on his shoulder and cradling his face in her other hand.

"Are you all right, dear?" she whispered to him. He simply smiled at her and patted her hand with his.

Nik glanced at Billy with raised eyebrows. This was bedside manner like they had never seen. She looked as if she were going to kiss him. Nik cleared his throat rather conspicuously.

Nurse Grace caught herself and stood bolt upright by the bed, adjusting her cap nervously. Billy smiled at her. They didn't have to worry about her saying a word to anyone of their presence here.

"It's all right, Grace," Rupert said. "These young gentlemen merely took a wrong turn and got lost."

"Rupert?" Billy asked, "Is your name Rupert Gould?"

The man looked at him with a slightly pained expression. He glanced at Grace, but she looked equally pained. After a long pause, he nodded.

"Mr. Gould, I must know if you've seen my uncle."

Grace spoke before Rupert could, "Young man, Mr. Gould is very ill and needs to rest. What is the meaning of coming in here and disturbing him this way?"

Rupert raised his hand to silence her.

"Grace, as I said, it's all right. Would you mind waiting outside for a moment?"

"Yes, Rupert, I would mind. Between yesterday's air raid and that strange doctor coming to see you with no warning, taking it upon himself to..."

Billy's jaw dropped.

"Janus has been here!"

"Who?" Grace asked.

Billy and Rupert traded serious glances.

Grace continued, "Does this have anything to do with that Guild you told me about?"

Billy snickered, "I guess Uncle Will's not the only one expanding the membership." This brought another stern glance from Rupert.

Nik chimed, "Well, it's like Mr. Franklin said. 'Three men can keep a secret if two of them are dead.'"

"So, how is old Ben?" Rupert asked, cracking a smile.

"He's fine," Billy said, "He asked about you, asked how you were doing."

"And you told him?"

"Uncle Will told him you were here." Billy continued, "Since we're on the subject, has my uncle been here?"

Rupert replied, "I'm afraid I haven't seen him; but Janus has certainly presented his credentials." As he said this he absently rubbed the inside of his right elbow.

"So, now what are we supposed to do?" Nik asked.

Billy was equally perplexed. "Why would the globe have been set to put us here? Why would Uncle Will do that?"

Rupert spoke up. "Perhaps it wasn't William."

Billy stood still for a moment, thinking about what Rupert said. Suddenly, he thrust his hand into his pocket and yanked out the watch.

"Nuts! We've just been sent down a rabbit trail!"

Nik stepped forward and asked, "What are you doing? Stop and think about what you are doing."

"We've got to get back to the house!"

"Young man," Rupert spoke in an even tone, "if you leave from here, you will not make it to William's home."

"What?"

"I'm assuming you refer to his home in England," Rupert continued, "because if you are, you won't be able to leave from here." With that, he reached up and switched on the lamp that stood next to the bed. It was only then that the boys realized how dark it had gotten. "Besides, it's a bit too late to use the watch now. You'll have to wait until tomorrow."

Billy hung his head in disgust and slipped the watch back into his pocket. Nik let out a deep sigh.

Rupert continued, "You'll need a place to stay tonight. I'm assuming you have made no such arrangements."

"You're assuming right," Billy conceded.

Rupert turned to Grace, who was sitting on the edge of his bed, listening intently.

"Do you think these boys might stay at your flat tonight?"

"Rupert," she said with a kidding smile, "I'm surprised you'd trust me alone with two young men in my flat. Unfortunately, my landlady would certainly not approve."

"Ah, there is that." Rupert paused to consider an alternative, and then spoke up. "There's a pub down the way called the Horse and Groom that hires rooms on the upper floor. You could stay there."

"Just one problem, Mr. Gould," Billy said.

"What's that?"

"We don't have any money. At least not any that we could spend here."

"Oh dear," Grace responded, "Perhaps I could give you something. Wait here."

With that, she exited the room, leaving Rupert and the boys alone.

"She's wonderful, isn't she?" Rupert mused.

"Yeah, great," Billy said, wondering what sort of trouble this woman was going to get into being involved with one of her patients, much less a member of the Guild.

Nik asked, "Why was she so upset about the watch before?"

"Ah," Rupert answered, "because of the nature of my condition, I am not permitted to have a watch. I guess they're afraid I'll take it apart and use the pieces to spring myself out of here." He laughed at his own statement. "But I'm not that easily thwarted. Grace was kind enough to loan me hers." With that, he reached under his pillow and drew out a small lady's wristwatch. He cradled it as lovingly as he had Billy's watch, smiling warmly as he held it to his ear.

"So tell me," Rupert continued, "you have Tempus Fugit. What about the other watches?"

Billy answered, "Well, Tempus Om... Tempus...uh... Oh, the one that says 'Time Heals All Wounds' was found with Marcus Straker. He smashed it to prevent Janus from getting it."

"Oh, no! Where is he?"

"In a mental institution."

Rupert pursed his lips. "I'm not surprised. The man was daft as a brush."

Billy glanced at Nik, and the two rolled their eyes.

Billy went on. "We figure Janus has one other one, but we're not sure about the fourth."

"Which brings you here."

Billy sighed, "I just want to find Uncle Will."

A moment later, Grace reentered the room. She approached Nik, who was standing closest to her, and reached inside her pocket. She brought out a few pounds and handed them to Nik.

"It should be enough to cover one night. You may have to share a bed."

Billy responded gratefully, "I just wish there was a way to repay you."

"Anything for Rupert's friends." She glanced lovingly at Rupert. "He can pay me back when he's able," she added with a giggle.

"Gentlemen," Rupert began, "once daybreak comes tomorrow, you'll need to go to the alley behind the Horse and Groom. There you will be able to reach William's house with the watch. One other thing I must tell you is to be very careful here. In case you are unaware, there is a war going on."

Rupert motioned to the window. Billy walked over to it and lifted the edge of the curtain. Although the sun had gone down, there was still enough light to see. He found himself on the second floor, so looking down, he saw stacks of sandbags everywhere. They were piled in front of every building he could see.

"If there is an air raid," Rupert added, "seek cover in the pub's cellar. I wish you every success."

After that, he gave them directions to the Horse and Groom and asked Grace to escort them out. They thanked him and wished him well.

The small room and narrow bed, made narrower by having to share, was a drastic departure from the accommodations at Uncle Will's house. Neither of the boys really slept. The room was bleak and plain, and it made Rupert's room at the hospital seem like a hotel room. The boys had managed to secure the room without drawing much attention to themselves. Most of the patrons in the pub downstairs were preoccupied either with news of the war or a game of darts. Eventually, the only sounds that trickled into their room were the sounds of the owner cleaning up the last of the bottles and glasses. Even that subsided at some point.

Although, it felt like he had never fallen asleep, Billy suddenly found himself being awakened by the wail of a siren. He rolled over to see Nik already out of bed and looking out the window. They saw huge white beams of light sweeping the night sky, pointing in all directions. Simultaneously, they remembered Rupert's instructions. At once, they bounded down the stairs into the pub. It was deserted and dark, making it impossible to find the entrance to the cellar. They dashed outside. There they could see one of the giant searchlights a few doors down the lane, slowly scanning back and forth. The constant wail of sirens filled their ears. Seeing no cover, Billy spun around to go back into the pub and ran headlong into a man who was exiting behind them.

The man was middle-aged and wore a sweater and, oddly enough to Billy, a helmet. The man was equally surprised by the encounter.

"What the devil are you boys doing out here?"

When Billy had finally collected himself, he realized that the man was the owner of the Horse and Groom, the same man that had rented them the room for the night.

"We were trying to find the cellar," Billy replied.

"Well, there really isn't any room in the cellar for all of us," the man said, "so follow me."

The man jogged to the house next door, which was obviously where he lived, with Billy and Nik close behind him. There they found the entrance to a cellar and took refuge there. A short, plump middle-aged woman who they assumed to be the man's wife met them. She was squatting against the stone wall, cradling a small, black fox terrier.

"You can stay here until it's over," he said. "I've got to get back." With that, he climbed the steps out of the cellar and was gone. Billy was about to make introductions when the dog suddenly wriggled free of its owner and bolted out the door and up the same steps. The woman struggled to her feet.

"Betsy! Betsy!" she called, running after the dog.

The boys followed her out. Suddenly, they heard a loud thump and felt the ground shudder under their feet. All the while, the sirens continued to wail. Once they reached the front garden of the house, they tried to locate the woman. She was chasing the dog into the street, which fortunately was deserted of vehicles. In the distance they could see her husband running toward the searchlight they had seen earlier. When he heard the woman calling for the dog, he stopped and wheeled around.

"Claudia!" he shouted over the sirens, "forget that bloody dog and take cover!" His command was immediately followed by a loud boom that shook the ground again. Billy finally realized that those were bombs falling and that they were getting closer. Nik grabbed Billy by the arm and spun him around.

"There!" He pointed toward the corner of a house across the road. Crouching low under a bush was the dog. The boys ran toward it.

"We found her!" Billy called to the woman. "Don't worry. We'll bring her back."

The woman continued to stand in the middle of the road. Another loud boom shook the night. By now, the man had made his way back to where she stood, goading her to return to the cellar.

"You boys forget that dog and get back here!" The couple had reached the edge of the front garden of their house. Billy looked up just as Nik was bending down to pick up the terrified animal. Suddenly, there was a bright flash. For the briefest of moments, Billy felt like he'd been hit in the face. He felt the sound as much as he heard it. It felt like his eardrums were coming out. He flew back and collided with Nik. The two tumbled over the bush, only to be stopped by the wall of the house behind it. They blacked out.

When Billy opened his eyes, it almost hurt to do so. He was bent into the most awkward position. He felt something poking him in the back. When he finally gathered the strength to roll over, he realized it was Nik's knee. Nik was coming to his senses about the same time. He was still clutching the dog. The two of them slowly rose to their feet and slapped what seemed like pounds of dust from their clothes. Billy's ears were ringing, and there was a bitter, gritty taste in his mouth. He spat gray mud on the ground. Soon, his ears were filled with the noises of people shouting and engines running. He tried to see through the thick smoke that seemed to cover everything. When he looked in the direction of the pub owner's house, he saw nothing but the broken remains of the front wall. A fire raged out of the crater behind it. He blinked a few times, trying to clear the smoke and dust from his eyes, but the image remained unchanged.

Billy and Nik slowly picked their way across the road, which was now littered with the smoking remains of the house. Billy's hearing was steadily improving, and he suddenly realized he was hearing a groaning sound from behind a large heap of rubble in what used to be the front garden. He ran to the top of the pile. Just behind it laid the man whose house this once was. He was half buried in pieces of broken stone and wood. It was hard to tell where his injuries were, because he was almost completely covered in blood. His left eye was forced shut from a massive injury to that side of his head. Billy rushed to his side. Nik soon came clambering down the heap to join him.

"Sir?" Billy said, taking the man's arm.

The man responded with a loud groan and glanced about wildly with his one functioning eye. When he was able to focus on Billy, he pleaded for help.

"Just rest easy," Billy assured. "We'll get you out of here."

Nik dropped the dog, and it scurried off around the side of the broken wall. The boys began to carefully pick pieces of rubble from the pile in an attempt to free their host. They made short work of uncovering him, but any attempt to move him resulted in a shriek of pain. They could hear the dog baying and whining from around the corner of the wall.

Billy motioned to Nik. "Go see what's wrong."

Nik slipped away carefully, and Billy took the man's hand to try and reassure him.

"Just relax. Help is on the way." What help, he thought to himself. Nik soon returned with a look of dismay.

"What's up?" Billy asked.

Nik was hesitant to say. He gestured for Billy to step away from the man. As Billy did so, Nik leaned toward him.

"She is dead. The man's wife is dead."

Billy closed his eyes and drew a breath. How was he going to tell this man without worsening his already critical condition? The man cried out in pain, and Billy rushed back to his side.

"It's all right. We're still here."

"Claudia!" the man called. "My Claudia!" He began to sob. He knew, Billy thought. He knew. The man began to wheeze and cough.

"C'mon mister," Billy pleaded, "You've got to hang on!"

The man strained to reach into his pocket. Billy saw him draw out a gold pocket watch. It was a bit smaller than his was. The man handed it to Billy.

"Open it," he whispered.

Billy snapped the cover open and looked at it. At first, it looked just like any other watch. It was, however, broken as result of the explosion. What shocked Billy was the tiny portrait fastened to the inside of the cover. It was the same picture that Uncle Will had placed inside his watch when they were in Norway. It was a picture of Aunt Catherine! Billy locked eyes with the man.

The man wheezed, "Tell my daughter...I love her." Billy's heart was racing. The man continued, "Tell her...her mum loves her too. Her name...is Catherine."

Billy dropped the watch in the rubble and took the man's hand.

"You can tell her yourself. You're going to make it." Billy sounded more pleading than reassuring. He turned to Nik.

"Get some help!"

Nik bounded down the pile of debris and took off toward the

searchlight. By now, people were beginning to appear in the street. Billy turned back to Aunt Catherine's father, and the man gazed skyward.

"I hope...she'll be...all right," he whispered, coughing blood as he spoke.

"She's fine," Billy said through the growing lump in his throat. "She's going to be okay. Trust me." This can't be happening, he thought.

The man reached with his free hand to pat Billy on the shoulder. His strength was gone, and his hand slid down Billy's chest until it landed in Billy's lap. He gasped, then relaxed in death.

Billy was beside himself. He felt sick to his stomach. He wanted to scream. He scarcely heard the noise of Nik and a group of others climbing up the rubble to offer help that was no longer needed. Once everyone else realized it was too late, Nik pulled Billy to his feet and led him to the pub next door. That building was relatively unscathed. The only damage was the broken windows on the side of the building that faced the house. They found a small wooden bench on the sidewalk near the pub's entrance. Billy slumped onto the bench with a blank expression. Nik simply put his hand on Billy's shoulder and did not speak. They sat there for quite a while, until darkness gave way to sunrise.

"We'd better get back," Nik said in a low tone.

Chapter Twenty-Four

Because of the overnight stay, they arrived back at Uncle Will's house about an hour after they had left. After what they had been through, they were certainly not prepared for what greeted them. The library was ransacked. The desk had been overturned, spilling its contents on the floor. The furniture was in disarray. Books had been pulled from the shelves and dumped just about everywhere. The boys were speechless.

"Billy! Nikolai!" The voice was unmistakably that of Aunt Catherine. The boys turned and saw her and Gwyneth approach from behind a tall oak cabinet. Aunt Catherine took Billy's hands and squeezed them as she breathed a silent prayer. Gwyneth stumbled into Nik's waiting arms and embraced him, resting her head on his shoulder. The fact that he was covered in dust didn't seem to even occur to her. He glanced apprehensively at Billy, but Billy simply nodded.

"We were so worried about you," Aunt Catherine said. "We're glad you're safe."

"What happened?" Billy asked, scanning the room in disbelief.

"We don't know," Aunt Catherine continued. "After you left this morning, your uncle brought us to visit the Radcliffes. I assumed that he would return here to wait for you. Mr. Radcliffe was kind enough to have his driver bring us home."

Billy responded, "So, you haven't seen Uncle Will since then."

"I'm afraid not."

Billy could see the worry in Aunt Catherine's eyes. He could also hear Gwyneth quietly sobbing into Nik's shoulder.

"Billy," Aunt Catherine asked, "what's happened to your suit? Are you hurt?"

Suddenly, Billy realized that, in addition to the dust, his shirt and jacket were stained with blood. He shot a glance at Nik, as if asking him what to say. Nik drew a breath and quietly led Gwyneth out of the library to the front sitting room.

"Billy, what happened?" Aunt Catherine pressed.

He felt sick to his stomach again, as a lump grew in his throat. He unconsciously stepped back. Aunt Catherine's eyes shifted downward. She sat softly on the end of the sofa, patting the cushion next to her.

"Sit down, Billy. Don't be afraid."

He reluctantly sat down. She knows, he thought to himself.

She said, "I noticed the globe was set for 1939."

Billy said nothing. He leaned forward and rested his elbows on his knees, letting his head hang down. She placed her hand on his shoulder. Tears of frustration welled in his eyes, and his hands began to shake. It was the same frustration he felt looking at Anastasia's picture in Uncle Will's book, the same frustration when Uncle Will told him they were going to let Mary Jane Kelly die.

"We were trying to find Uncle Will," he sobbed. "We ended up in a hospital. Then we had to spend the night in a room at some local bar." He paused to catch his breath.

"The Horse and Groom." Aunt Catherine's voice was soft and deliberate. "My father's pub."

Billy drew a deep breath. "There was an air raid. There were bombs." He sobbed some more.

"It's all right, Billy," Aunt Catherine whispered. Her voice was breaking.

"I tried to help him, but I didn't know what to do!" Billy said, pounding his knee with his fist.

Aunt Catherine leaned forward, put his arm around Billy, and drew him closer to her.

"It wasn't your fault, Billy."

"But I could have stopped it!"

"It wasn't for you to stop."

Billy turned and glared at her through reddened eyes.

"Do you realize what you're saying?!"

She smiled ever so slightly at him and answered, "Yes. I do. Those events are in God's hands. They don't take Him by surprise."

Billy thought for a moment, and then took the watch from his pocket.

"Why would He give us the power to change it if we're not supposed to?"

Aunt Catherine was silent.

"He said he loved you," Billy said softly, "and that your mother loved you, too."

Aunt Catherine wiped a tear from her eye.

Billy continued, "He showed me a picture of you that he kept in his watch." He sighed. "I wish I'd thought to at least bring that back."

Aunt Catherine sniffed, leaned back, and reached inside her collar. As Billy observed, she drew out one end of a long gold chain that was looped around her neck. At the end of the loop was a battered gold watch. Billy's eyes widened as he recognized it as the one her father had shown him. She held it up and opened the cover. The crystal was cracked and the hands were frozen, no doubt at the exact moment the bomb had hit.

"A neighbor found it in the rubble," she explained. "I've kept it just as it was found."

Billy asked, "Will you ever get it fixed?"

"No. It was my father's watch. Time no longer matters for him now. He lives outside of it."

Billy and Aunt Catherine both leaned back on the sofa. He rested his head on her shoulder. Although he was relieved of this burden, he still felt an overbearing frustration.

"I guess we both lost someone we cared about."

"Oh, Billy," Aunt Catherine replied, "I've been meaning to tell you how sorry I was to hear about Anastasia. I know how much she meant to you."

There was a long silence as aunt and nephew stared ahead at the disarray around them. Then Aunt Catherine spoke up.

"It is good to see that someone else has found someone to care for."

Billy glanced at her, not sure of what she meant. She nodded toward the corridor that led to the front sitting room. There, silhouetted against the light coming in from the window, Gwyneth sat with her head resting on Nik's shoulder. Nik's head was resting against hers. Billy sat up. He turned and looked apprehensively at Aunt Catherine, who simply smiled.

Suddenly, her expression turned serious.

"Billy, did you ever find Uncle William while you were gone?"

Billy's mouth dropped open. He had nearly forgotten.

Aunt Catherine quickly rose to her feet, as did Billy. He called to Nik to cut short his little "visit" and get changed to return to Cannon Falls. Then it occurred to him that he did not have the orbital displacement calculator. He looked at the globe.

"Do you have any idea how to work that thing?" he asked his aunt. She shrugged and shook her head.

"We'll just have to wing it."

In a moment, the boys were back in their own clothes and standing at the window. Billy aimed the watch at the sun.

"Do be careful, Billy," Aunt Catherine said.

"Yes," Gwyneth repeated, "please do be careful. Both of you." She looked at Nik.

Chapter Twenty-Five

The watch placed them back in Katter's field, but at the opposite corner. Fortunately, they were still well concealed by the high corn. Once they regained their bearings, they made for the path they took out of the field to reach Billy's house. As they walked along the edge of the field, Nik suddenly clutched Billy's arm and pointed into the distance. Billy looked forward and spotted a lone figure standing in their path. It was Janus, and he stood there grinning.

"I was beginning to wonder if you would show."

Billy glanced all around, trying to find a way of escape. At once, he grabbed Nik by the arm and dragged him into the cornrows.

"You stupid boy!" Janus shouted. "How long do you really think you can hide from me?"

Billy could hear Janus rushing into the corn, but Billy could not see him. That's good, he thought, because if we can't see him, he can't see us. The boys continued deeper into the field, changing direction constantly. At the same time, they were trying to make their way to the opposite edge of the field, hoping to make an end run around Janus. It was slow going, trying not to make any sounds that would help Janus locate them.

"You may as well give up, Billy," Janus taunted.

Billy ignored him. The boys continued their trek through the field.

Janus shouted again. "You're forcing my hand, Billy. Don't make me do something we'll both regret."

Yeah, right, Billy thought, as if Janus would regret anything.

The boys continued to move slowly through the field, all the while looking in all directions to make sure Janus wasn't close by. Billy's ears strained to hear Janus moving through the corn. They were getting closer to the clearing where they were headed before their encounter.

"Billy, I think I should tell you that she's alive!" Janus said.

Billy stopped cold. He knew full well whom Janus was talking about. Nik stopped and looked back at Billy, studying his face carefully.

Janus continued, "Did you really think I would be that heartless?

I'm not the monster your uncle believes me to be."

Billy stood still, listening intently.

"She's fine, Billy," Janus said. "She's somewhere safe. Let me take you to her."

Billy started to pace between two rows of corn. Nik could see that he was agitated, and started to try and reassure him. Billy recoiled and started to walk toward the sound of Janus' voice. Nik seized him by the arm and shook his head emphatically. Billy tore his arm free and grabbed Nik by the shirt.

"What am I supposed to do," he hissed, "leave her with him?"

He turned to go. This time, Nik threw his arms around Billy's midsection and pushed him to the ground. Pinning Billy, Nik leaned close to his face.

"Think about what you are doing. He's lying. He has to be."

Nik's action shocked Billy to his senses, but he still protested.

"But I can't just leave her..."

"She is gone, Billy."

Billy stared into Nik's eyes with a pleading expression, but Nik would not relent. Finally, Billy relaxed and rose to his feet. The two continued until they reached the edge of the field.

Just as Billy stepped out of the cornrows, he was sent reeling by the impact of a fist against his face. He barely caught the sight of a black-sleeved arm attached to the fist. As he hit the mud, he felt a hand fish through his pocket and remove the watch.

"That was too easy," Janus laughed. All Billy could do was shut his eyes in defeat. How could this be happening, he thought. Janus immediately put several yards distance between himself and the boys.

"Your insane uncle didn't count on this. I knew Marcus would try to get a message to him. It didn't take much to figure out what he was up to. But then, why am I wasting my time talking to you about it? I've got more important things to do."

Billy couldn't take it anymore. He rose to his knees and screamed out loud through clenched teeth, pounding the bare soil with his fists. Nik stood motionless. Janus turned back and smiled, as if satisfied at Billy's outburst.

"Don't take it too hard, young man," he said. "Your uncle was crazy, but he gave me quite a run for my money. He was a smart man."

"What do you mean 'was?'" Nik hissed.

"He just wasn't fast enough. Right about now, Peters, my associate, is on his way back to your uncle's estate in England with a little "present."

The boys' faces froze in horror. After hearing what Uncle Will had said about the things Janus was trying to get his hands on, they hardly dared to imagine what sort of "present" he meant. Janus smiled, turned, and pointed his watch toward the sun. Just as he did so, there was a rustling sound in the corn. Suddenly, Uncle Will stumbled from behind a row of stalks. He was wearing, not the type of clothes he wore in 1889, but his usual trousers and shirt with his tattered old cardigan sweater. Regaining his balance, he adjusted his glasses, then turned and smiled at the boys. They were speechless. Janus was equally shocked. By now, the hole had opened and stood hovering in front of him; but rather than make his escape, he turned to face Uncle Will.

"You just don't know when to quit, Sheppard!"

"Alexander, I thought you'd be happy to see me," replied Uncle Will with a characteristically toothy grin. "Oh, by the way, I'm afraid Peters didn't get to deliver your package to my house. Anyway, I sent him on his way a short while ago."

"What?!" Billy and Nik gasped.

"Actually," Uncle Will continued, taking his computer from his pocket, "he's gone to Siberia. Tunguska to be exact. 1908. If the blast doesn't get him, the cold will. I guess that's the last we'll see of him."

"A minor inconvenience, Sheppard!" Janus shouted. The fact that his face was turning red betrayed his true rage. "He was only getting in the way! I would have finished him off myself, sooner of later! Now, if you'll excuse me, I don't have time to chat anymore. History awaits!" Janus turned back toward the hole.

"Janus!" Uncle Will shouted, taking a clenched fist from his pocket. "Tempus neminem exspectat!"

"What did you say?!" Janus spun around once more. Even Billy and Nik were bewildered. Not another hand grenade, Billy thought.

Uncle Will raised his fist and opened it. A large gold disk fell from his hand. The gold chain to which it was attached stopped its fall. Billy instantly recognized it as the medallion that Gwyneth wore around her neck. That's what was missing when he saw her that morning. Until then, she had always worn it. As the sun reflected off it, it spun around and he could plainly see the inscription on the back:

"Tempus Neminem Exspectat"

Uncle Will continued, "Time waits for no man! And your time is up!"

At once, Uncle Will snapped open the medallion to reveal that it was actually another watch. Uncle Will knew all along where the other watch was. He was hiding it in plain sight, around his daughter's neck! Its crystal cover immediately captured the sunlight. As a circle of color began to form, it started to merge with the hole that Janus had already opened. Janus' eyes widened.

"Are you crazy?!"

Uncle Will laughed. "As a matter of fact—yes!"

Whenever Billy had seen such a watch being used, he always noticed a slight ringing sound in the air. This time, he heard an earsplitting shriek. His uncle leaned toward him.

"You boys had better get out of here!"

"But Uncle Will, I thought you were never supposed to..."

The old man turned his head and glared at the boys with a look of rage on his face that Billy had never seen in all the years he had known him.

"RUN!!"

The two holes had completely merged and formed a large black sphere. Billy and Nik jumped into action and sprinted with all their strength down the dirt path and up the hill. The wind began to blow hard against their faces as the shrieking turned to a roar. Stalks of corn began to pull out of the ground and fly toward the place where they had stood moments ago. Billy looked over his shoulder to see Nik at his heels. He looked farther back and saw Janus flat on his face, clawing the soft earth. A rusted old York rake that was imbedded in that corner of the field suddenly flew over Janus' head, missing him narrowly and disappearing into the void. Instantly, he was lifted up and drawn toward the black sphere. No sooner had it consumed him, than Billy saw his uncle leaning away from it with his heels dug into the ground. Uncle Will turned and looked at Billy through narrowed eyes. His arm was lifted in a vain attempt to shield his face from the flying debris. He smiled at Billy, and then disappeared into it as well.

Billy was too frightened to stop. He continued to run toward the edge of the field, gasping desperately for air despite the growing lump in his throat. His vision began to blur as his eyes filled with tears. He could hear Nik's feet pounding the soil behind him. Within seconds, the roar had stopped, and the rushing wind with it. As they reached the crest of the hill, they stopped and looked back. All that remained of that corner of the field was a dark, barren circle, about fifty feet wide. The corn was gone, the soil was gone, and worst of all, Uncle Will was gone. All three of the remaining watches had gone with him. Billy stood gasping for breath between sobs. Nik put his arm on Billy's shoulder and tried to catch his own breath. Billy dropped to his knees in exhaustion and despair.

Chapter Twenty-Six

Billy and Nik sat in silence on the crest of the hill. Close to an hour had passed when the darkening sky reminded them to head for home. The sun had already dipped below the trees. Soon they had arrived at Nik's house.

"So what are you going to tell your parents about...?" Nik hesitated to mention Uncle Will's name.

"I don't know," responded Billy, with very little emotion.

"I wonder what really happened back there," Nik wondered.

Billy stared at him coldly. "I think it's pretty obvious what happened."

"I'm sorry Billy. I did not mean to..."

"Forget it."

Nik turned and walked up the driveway to his house.

Billy continued on his way home. His mind raced as Nik's question echoed through it. What would he tell his parents? Would they even believe him? His mind was so consumed with questions that he nearly walked past his own home. Only the sound of his mother's voice grabbed his attention.

"Billy!" She sounded very upset. "Where have you been? Come inside. Something awful has happened!"

You're telling me, Billy thought as he crossed the front yard and ascended the steps. His mother had already gone back inside. He felt sick to his stomach, still trying to figure out what to say or do next. As he entered the house, his mother paced frantically across the foyer.

"We got a call from the hospital," she sputtered. "Your uncle is missing. They think he may have escaped. Your father just went down there to see what can be done." Suddenly, she stopped in front of him. "Billy! What on earth happened to your face?"

Billy had forgotten the large bruise on his cheek. He thrust his hand up in front of it, trying to think of an explanation.

"Uh...I got hit with a football!" he blurted out. "I'm okay."

"You should be more careful," his mother replied, placing her hand on his chin and shifting his head to the side. Billy winced.

"You'd better put some ice on that."

"Mom..." he began.

"Oh, it's just terrible!" She ignored him. "I should have known something like this might happen. I was wrong to send him there!"

Carolyn Maxwell entered the living room and slumped into Steve's big, brown recliner. She leaned forward and put her head in her hands. Billy stood alone in the foyer, still trying to get up the courage to talk to his mother. He gave up. She was in no condition to hear it, he thought. He went downstairs to the workshop. At least he still had the key.

Once the door closed behind him, he turned and scanned the room. He looked at the junk piled under the workbench; the wire recorder, the tools, the life ring from the R.M.S. Titanic, the autographed picture of Howard Hughes, and finally Anastasia's Kodak Brownie, still holding the undeveloped photographs of Billy and Nik. He wondered for a moment what other pictures she had taken with that camera. What else had she seen? Who else would she have wanted to remember? With a heavy feeling in his chest, Billy slid onto one of the chairs at the table.

A moment later, Billy could hear the telephone ringing upstairs. The first ring had barely faded when he heard his mother's footsteps moving from the living room to the kitchen. He figured it was his father on the other end, or perhaps the police. Billy got up from the chair and opened the door, listening intently, trying to determine what his mother was saying. While he listened, the doorbell rang.

"Billy!" his mother called, "Billy, please get the door!"

He dragged himself up the stairs, still wondering what he would tell his parents. Upon reaching the door, he looked through the screen and saw a man in a brown uniform. The man had thinning gray hair that protested all efforts to keep it combed. His gray eyes peeked over the tops of his thick eyeglasses. Covering his mouth was a thick black mustache. The man held a small box in one hand and a clipboard in the other. Billy cracked open the screen door.

"I have a package for a Mister Billy Maxwell," the man said. His voice was throaty to the point of being comical. He spoke in an exaggerated Southern accent, quite out of place in the middle of Minnesota.

Billy hesitantly took the box that the man presented and tucked it under his arm. Then, he took the clipboard and signed his name where the man indicated. He thanked the man, turned, and let the door snap shut behind him. Glancing over his shoulder, he received a wink from the departing deliveryman. Before he could react, the man was back in his van. Billy shook his head and took the box down to the workshop.

Closing the door, Billy sat back down and took the box in his hands. After staring at it for a moment, he tore the lid open and looked inside. It was filled with strips of shredded newsprint, which were yellow and brittle and smelled like a dusty attic. The stuffing obscured the actual contents of the box, so Billy began to dig. The item he pulled out was a large photograph. It was a black and white print of a group of people seated at large round table in what appeared to be a restaurant.

Much to Billy's astonishment, one of the people at the table was Uncle Will. He was seated at the center of the group, wearing a tuxedo. Seated next to him was Aunt Catherine, dressed in a dark colored formal evening gown. There were others in the photograph that Billy recognized, but not because he had ever met them. He recognized them from the old movies his parents liked to watch on television. John Wayne sat to the left of Uncle Will, also dressed in a tuxedo and smoking a cigarette. Next to him sat Charlton Heston. To the right of Aunt Catherine sat Jimmy Stewart. There were a few other people sitting at the table that he didn't recognize.

What captured his attention next would have been barely noticeable to the casual observer. At the very left edge of the photograph, almost hidden in the background, was a small table. There were two young women sitting at the table. One of them was facing the camera, looking, it seemed, right into Billy's eyes. It was Anastasia. She was alive, and she was safe with Uncle Will. Billy's heart raced. He studied the picture for several minutes with wide-eyed amazement, almost forgetting the box in his lap.

Once he put the picture on the table, he reached into the box again. This time he took out what looked like another photograph. It was actually a postcard. The picture on the front of it showed a nightclub called the 'Brown Derby.' Billy immediately flipped it over to find a short handwritten message:

Dear Billy,
Having a good time.
Wish you were here!
Your Favorite Uncle.

Billy's mouth hung wide open as he read the message over and over to make sure he wasn't imagining it. He reached into the box again, pulling the remaining stuffing out in one handful. Sitting in the bottom of the box was an all too familiar gold watch, bearing an all too familiar inscription:

"Tempus Fugit"

Just for the Record

Ben Franklin really did say, "Three men can keep a secret if two of them are dead." It was likely published in Poor Richard's Almanac.

There really was a Rupert Gould, who did extensive research and restoration work on John Harrison's marine chronometers. He really did suffer a nervous breakdown following the start of World War II (his third), and spent some time in an institution. In the 1930's and 1940's, he appeared in a few BBC educational radio broadcasts, most notably "The Brains Trust."

There also really was a James Maybrick, who lived near Liverpool, England in 1889. He was reported to have died of arsenic poisoning; and his wife was tried and convicted of his murder. Her guilt or innocence is still debated. Several years ago, a diary surfaced which was claimed to be that of Maybrick. In the diary, the writer claims to be Jack the Ripper. (Note: Maybrick's family crest bore the inscription "Tempus Omnia Relevat.")

During the testing of America's first jet fighter, at Muroc Dry Lake Bed (later Edwards AFB), the test pilot did in fact take a gorilla mask, derby hat, and cigar on test flights. Base psychologists had no trouble convincing other pilots that they had not really seen this secret new aircraft.

For years, it was speculated that Anastasia, the youngest daughter of Tsar Nicholas II, escaped murder at the hands of the Bolsheviks. This decades old theory was supposedly put to rest a few years ago, when it was claimed that DNA testing of remains found at the abandoned mine where the royal family was buried accounted for all members. Incidentally, one of Anastasia's favorite hobbies was taking pictures with her Kodak Brownie.

The story of Corrie Ten Boom and her father, Casper, is told by Corrie herself in the book "The Hiding Place." They really did have a secret room in their house for hiding Jews from the Nazis. They were arrested in 1944 and sent to concentration camps. As a result of a clerical error, Corrie was released from the Ravensbrouk camp one week before all the women in her age group were scheduled to be terminated.

In March of 1998, it was actually reported in Time Magazine that high-level secret documents, classified UMBRA, were stolen from the office of the U.S. State Department's executive secretary the previous month. The man who stole the documents simply walked into the office, opened a diplomatic pouch containing the papers, and walked out unchallenged. His identity remains a mystery.

In November of 1939, a mysterious package arrived at the office of the British Naval Attaché in Oslo, Norway. The package contained several German weapon designs that were so advanced, at first the Allies thought they were a hoax. These weapons included radar-guided bombs and cruise missiles. The package became known as the Oslo Report. It was addressed from "a well-wishing scientist."

In June of 1908, there was an unexplained explosion in the sky over Tunguska, Siberia. It was seen and heard as far away as Moscow. It leveled thousands of acres of forest. While the damage resembled that of an atomic bomb, scientists theorize that a comet or large meteor may have caused it.

"Linqua tuas sedes alienque litora quaere, O juneus.
Major rerum tibi nascitur ordo."

—Petronius

About the Author

Curt Yengst is a professional broadcast engineer who currently resides in Eastern Pennsylvania with his wife and two small children. A Jersey boy by birth, Curt has lived in as varied places as Minnesota and North Carolina; so he is clearly no stranger to culture shock. Curt is also a born-again Christian and has spent the last decade working in the Christian broadcast industry. He likes to describe himself as one of those rare people who get to make a living engaging in their hobbies.

Curt is the owner of Zerro House Productions, a small project studio and production company. An occasional songwriter, Curt uses his studio as another of his creative outlets.

Being an engineer, he is endlessly fascinated with all things technical. He credits (or blames) this fascination with his being a "behind-the-scenes" kind of guy. Curt says he would rather be the one behind the camera than in front of it, on the control-room side of the glass than on the studio side. He admits that most of his heroes are individuals that most people have never heard of.

His literary tastes tend to lean in that direction, and he usually enjoys reading non-fiction of a technical or historical nature. His interests, aside from audio engineering, include collecting pocket watches, building dollhouses for the girls in his family, military aircraft, and anything and everything pertaining to the U.S. Navy Blue Angels. He also enjoys spending time with his family.

Tempus Fugit is Curt's first novel, but with all the ideas he has banging around in his head, it won't be his last.

Printed in the United States
52249LVS00007B/268-294

9 781594 262227